"I also have a problem, Alice," Thanos said, his eyes boring into hers with an intensity that sent a shiver down her spine.

"And it occurs to me that we could be of use to one another."

Her eyes flared. Without knowing any details, she knew she shouldn't get her hopes up. And yet it felt like...a light in the dark.

"How so?"

"My brother suggested last night that I should give Kosta Carenedes exactly what he wants."

"You're going to stop getting photographed by paparazzi?" Alice prompted, a hint of skepticism in her words, because the media loved Thanos and his antics.

"I'm not sure that's possible. But I'm going to give them the right thing to photograph."

"What do you mean?"

"If Kosta wants me to settle down, then I'll do just that. I'll get married."

It was so absurd that Alice laughed. "You're getting married?"

"That depends."

"On...?"

"On if you'll agree to be my wife."

Clare Connelly

———

BRIDE BEHIND THE BILLION-DOLLAR VEIL

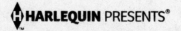
HARLEQUIN PRESENTS®

Recycling programs
for this product may
not exist in your area.

ISBN-13: 978-1-335-53881-9

Bride Behind the Billion-Dollar Veil

First North American publication 2019

Printed in U.S.A.

Clare Connelly was raised in small-town Australia among a family of avid readers. She spent much of her childhood up a tree, Harlequin romance book in hand. Clare is married to her own real-life hero and they live in a bungalow near the sea with their two children. She is frequently found staring into space—a surefire sign she is in the world of her characters. She has a penchant for French food and ice-cold champagne, and Harlequin novels continue to be her favorite-ever books. Writing for Harlequin Presents is a long-held dream. Clare can be contacted via clareconnelly.com or on her Facebook page.

Books by Clare Connelly

Harlequin Presents

Bought for the Billionaire's Revenge
Innocent in the Billionaire's Bed
Her Wedding Night Surrender
Bound by the Billionaire's Vows
Spaniard's Baby of Revenge

Secret Heirs of Billionaires

Shock Heir for the King

Christmas Seductions

Bound by Their Christmas Baby
The Season to Sin

Crazy Rich Greek Weddings

The Greek's Billion-Dollar Baby

Visit the Author Profile page
at Harlequin.com for more titles.

For Penny Jordan, whose beautiful, sensual, romantic Harlequin novels have given me hours and hours of romance-reading pleasure, not to mention a certainty that dreams really can come true.

PROLOGUE

Twelve years ago

'LISTEN TO ME.'

Thanos looked up at his brother, barely able to see him through the fog of rage and disbelief that shrouded his every thought and feeling.

'We will get it back.'

Thanos gripped the pen in his hand, returning his attention to the imperious black line at the bottom of the contract. A contract for the sale of Petó, the company their grandfather, Nicholas Stathakis, had built from the ground up. The company Thanos had learned to operate at his grandfather's knee. The company that meant everything to him.

'No.' He dropped the pen to the boardroom table, extending to his full six and a half feet, striding across the room with a ramrod-straight back.

He knew his half-brother was watching him, and he knew Leonidas was feeling the same sense of outrage and disbelief. Only Leonidas was somehow better at processing this. He was calm, outwardly, even as their world crumbled around them, whereas Thanos wanted to torch the building on his way out.

He braced his palms on the floor-to-ceiling glass, looking out on downtown Athens. All of this they had once commanded.

All of this, their father had destroyed.

'We will get it back, Thanos,' Leo repeated, with urgency. 'But we must sell it for now.'

Nausea split Thanos's side. Sell it? Sell the jewel in their grandfather's business empire? Because their father had tied the company to the mafia?

Thanos ground his teeth together, locking his jaw intently. He wanted to say there was another way. He wanted to fix this. To make it better. And suddenly he was eight years old again, watching his mother walk away. He was eight years old and knowing himself to be the instrument of a family's breakdown. He was eight years old and everything in this world was his fault. But this was so much worse.

Nicholas had trusted Thanos with Petó, and he'd been careless. He'd trusted Dion Stathakis— their father—when he should have seen what was happening right beneath his nose.

What could he do now?

'I cannot bear to think of someone else running his business.' Thanos's voice cracked with the strength of his emotions.

'Do you think I can?' Leonidas growled, and Thanos turned to face his brother then, their eyes meeting with complete understanding. This situation was wrong. Wrong in every way.

Leonidas softened his expression a little. 'But this is the best possibility we could have hoped for. Kosta Carinedes wants Petó. His plan to fold it into his own logistics empire are sound, so too the rebranding he envisages. Petó will live on, Thanos, and it will continue to prosper.'

Thanos's stomach clenched. 'But not by our hands.'

'No.' Leonidas's eyes glittered in acknowledgement of that.

'I will not live in a world where this company is not mine, Leonidas. One day, one way or another, Petó will be ours again.'

Leonidas nodded slowly but Thanos wasn't satisfied. 'Swear it to me, Leo. Swear to me now that we will right this wrong—and all our father's wrongs—even if it takes us the rest of our lives.'

Leonidas expelled a soft, low breath. 'I swear it. But you must sign the contract now.'

Thanos nodded, knowing his brother to be correct. Still, he glared at the paper as though it were a writhing tangle of snakes at his feet. He lifted the pen with difficulty and hovered it over the page, his perennial tan paled to straw in that moment.

He scrawled his name on the page and silently swore to himself, once more, that this wasn't the end.

This wasn't over—not by a long shot. Petó was a part of his blood and his DNA, and it always would be.

CHAPTER ONE

ALICE TOOK A full ten seconds to remember who she was and what she was doing. For a moment, the appearance of one man had managed to skittle everything from her mind: her job, her responsibilities; the mountain of medical bills she had in her handbag waiting for her to wade through at lunch time; the credit card that was almost maxed, and the fact this temp position would be finishing in two weeks, meaning she'd yet again need to find a job; her mother's worsening condition and Alice's inability to find a proper long-term solution for her care. Every second of every day those considerations pursued her, but for a moment, with the sound of the elevator doors opening to the top floor of the glass and steel monolith that was Stathakis Towers, she found the chatter of her mind was silenced and all she could do was stare.

Her almond-shaped brown eyes tracked his progress across the office, her pulse hammering her body from the inside out, the closer he came to her desk.

Thanos Stathakis was here. In his office. In Manhattan.

Despite the fact she'd temped for the man for five months, she hadn't once laid eyes on him, outside the endless stream of photos that littered the Internet. Photos of him invariably in a state of undress, relaxed, surrounded by a bevy of supermodels and actresses, partying, drinking, living the kind of life Alice could barely imagine.

The kind of life her father had also adored. The thought should have been sobering, but it wasn't. She was almost mesmerised by the sight of him in the flesh.

Thanos Stathakis wasn't just a man.

He was a legend.

His success in business was renowned—alongside his brother, he'd turned a crumbling business into an empire once more, like a powerful phoenix rising from the ashes of scandal and failure. But it was more than that. Thanos Stathakis was unlike anyone she'd ever known—in person, it was easy to see why the world's media was obsessed with him.

If there was a mould for tall, dark and handsome then Thanos had certainly broken it. He was broad-shouldered, slim-hipped, with strength and charisma in every long stride of his powerful legs. Unlike the photographs she'd seen of him, he wore a suit now, navy blue with a crisp white shirt that only served to emphasise the depth of his tan. His eyes were caramel-coloured and rimmed in thick, curling black lashes, so he looked almost as though he'd worked overtime with a mascara wand. He was the very image of the billionaire magnate she knew him to be, with the exception of his hair, which was somehow wild and untamed, as though he'd stepped straight off a speedboat on the Riviera and into the doors of this Manhattan monolith.

She stared at him because she couldn't help it, and even when his eyes jerked to hers, she didn't look away. Not for several long, compelling seconds.

His lips curled in what could have been a smile, or could have been derision, and then he stopped close enough to her desk for Alice to hold her breath.

'You're the temp?'

It was enough to jolt her back into the present—and who she was to him. The temp! As if she hadn't been keeping his life running seamlessly these past five months, since his regular assistant had been on leave.

'Alice, yes.'

'Alice.' He nodded, as if it didn't matter, and in a way that made her absolutely certain he'd have forgotten her name again in an instant.

Except he didn't turn and walk away. He continued to stare at her in a way that set her pulse racing, so she had to forcibly remind herself that he generally occupied himself with glamorous models, that there would be nothing in her somewhat plain face to cause him to stare like this. No, he must have another reason for looking into her eyes as though he'd seen her before.

He blinked then, like severing a thread, his dark lashes closing against his cheeks, forming perfect fans for the briefest of seconds before he opened his eyes and speared her with his intent gaze.

'Print the file on P & A Industries. I have a meeting in ten minutes.'

He spun on his heel and stalked towards the office to her left—an office she'd only been into once or twice since taking up this role. It was his office, and he hadn't been in New York the whole time she'd been at Stathakis Corp.

It was the final straw in rousing Alice back to reality.

Years ago, she'd looked at another man with that same deer-in-the-headlights sense of drowning and she'd come to regret it hugely. She'd fallen for Clinton's practised flirtation, hook, line, and sinker, and learned a valuable lesson— she wouldn't fall for another man's easy charms, ever again. And Thanos Stathakis was not in the realm of Clinton. Thanos was…bigger and somehow more dangerous.

She had no business staring at him as though he were the second coming.

She pushed back from her desk, following behind him. 'A meeting, sir?'

He opened the door, moving into the enormous space without turning the lights on, so it was Alice who flicked the switch and brought the overheads to life.

Like the rest of the building, this large room had a Scandinavian feel, with light timber furniture, pale walls and a cream carpet. The artwork was minimalist, the light fittings modern and striking. His desk sat against one wall with a state-of-the-art computer atop it and a piece of expensive art behind it; across the room, framed perfectly by floor-to-ceiling windows that showcased an incredible view of Manhattan, was a boardroom table large enough to accommodate twenty-two people.

'Mmm…' He made a noise of agreement, shrugging out of his jacket and placing it carelessly across the back of his chair. The movement only served to highlight the breadth of his shoulders and arms that looked to have been sculpted by God's own hand. Her lips parted and she stared—she knew she was staring but almost for the first time in Alice's life her self-control was nowhere to be seen.

'You know,' he drawled with a sinful smile pulling at those impossibly strong lips. 'That thing where people come to the same place at the same time to discuss a prearranged schedule of topics?'

She blinked, embarrassment shifting through her, and she was glad then that she didn't blush easily. 'I know what a meeting is,' she said softly, the fact he was teasing her setting off a thousand fires in the depth of her soul. 'I just meant it's not in your diary.'

Something flashed in his expression—triumph? Wariness?—and then he nodded curtly. 'It was arranged this morning. Kosta Carinedes happens to be in New York so I thought it was a good opportunity to…see him.'

Alice nodded. 'Fine. How many people will be at the meeting?' She was already slipping back into her professional groove, thinking of how quickly she could alert the catering team to send up refreshments, how many copies of documents she'd need to print.

'Just him and me. And you,' he added, as an afterthought. 'In case I need anything throughout.'

She nodded. 'I'll have the kitchen send up some sandwiches—'

'That won't be necessary. Just coffee. Strong and black.'

Alice nodded again. She remembered the handover notes that had been left for her, which described in detail how Thanos Stathakis liked to take his coffee.

'Fine.'

'You'll print the file?'

She nodded. 'Yes, sir.'

She was almost at the door when his voice stilled her. 'Alice?'

She spun around to face him once more, catching a slight frown on those sculpted lips. 'I don't like being called "sir".'

'I'm sorry, si—'

'Thanos,' he insisted.

'Thanos.' His name was bewitching on her lips. She said it and immediately wanted to say it again and again. She said it mentally as she printed the files he'd requested, and as she made a pot of Greek coffee, carrying it carefully into his office. He was on the phone when she entered. She busied herself arranging the documents in place, trying to ignore the sensation of heat that travelled the length of her spine as he hurled words in his native Greek, the words like a sunset after a storm, impossibly bright and intriguing.

She retreated from his office without noticing

the way his eyes followed her, scooping up her laptop and a bottle of water, before making her way to the boardroom table.

When she entered this time, he was no longer on the phone. 'My brother sometimes thinks I cannot tie my shoes without him,' he said, but the words were tinged with amusement. He stood, stretching his arms over his head, yawning and smothering it with his hand.

This was a man who was supremely confident. How Alice envied him that! She had worked hard to appear strong and put-together, to look as though she'd outgrown the wounds of her past, but she knew she came across as cold and aloof most of the time, even when that strength came out of a need to protect a too vulnerable heart.

It seemed unlikely Thanos had ever felt a hint of self-doubt in his life.

Except it wasn't just confidence that oozed out of him. It was determination. She felt it emanating from him in waves and it held her in her spot for a moment, even as she knew she should go back to her own desk, to be waiting for Kosta Carinedes when he arrived.

'Is there anything I should know before this meeting?' she heard herself asking instead, reluctant to take herself from his office.

'No. It is a simple matter. He has something I want; I intend to buy it back today.'

The words were clipped, his expression business-like.

'I anticipate the meeting will conclude quickly enough.'

'Fine.' Alice checked everything was in order and without looking in Thanos's direction—perhaps out of fear that she might not easily be able to look away again—she returned to her own desk.

Not five minutes later, the lift doors pinged open and a man emerged. Older than Alice had expected, with a lined face and a kind smile, his hair was greying, his body a little stooped, dressed in a suit that looked bespoke with expensive leather shoes.

'Stathakis?' he said as he approached Alice's desk.

'This way, sir.' She stood, gesturing towards Thanos's office. At the door, she knocked twice and then pushed it inwards, stepping back to allow the older Greek man to precede her.

From her vantage point, she saw the way Thanos's body momentarily tensed and the determination she'd observed moments earlier was back, a palpable force in the room.

Kosta spoke first, in Greek, and Thanos returned the greeting in their native tongue before switching to English.

'Alice, my assistant, doesn't speak Greek.'

Kosta threw a look over his shoulder and then shrugged. 'Perhaps you can tell me why I have been summoned here?'

Even that was a telling statement. Thanos Stathakis had the power to summon just about anyone to his office, and it was a power he had flexed this morning.

'You don't know?'

Kosta shrugged his shoulders. 'I presume it has something to do with P & A?'

Thanos's stare was direct. 'Yes.' He gestured towards the table. 'Please, take a seat.'

The old man hesitated for a moment and then did as he'd been bid, moving to a chair on one side of the table and settling himself into it. Alice watched as he lifted the coffee to his lips, sipping it, then returning the cup to the saucer at the same time Thanos took a seat at the head of the table.

'You've received my offer?' That confidence was back, brimming and blinding. Alice stared covertly at Thanos as she settled herself at the end of the boardroom table, flipping her laptop open and pulling up a blank Word document to take notes.

'My lawyer advised me of it,' the older man remarked with another shrug of his shoulders, in what Alice was recognising as a trademark gesture.

'And?'

Kosta expelled a soft breath. 'Did my silence not answer your question?'

Alice jerked her gaze to Thanos on autopilot. He didn't visibly react to Kosta's question. 'Silence can mean many things.'

Kosta's lips compressed. 'Not in this instance.'

'You want to sell.' It was a question and yet Thanos delivered it more as a statement, one that was laced with iron.

'To the right buyer, yes.' Kosta took another sip of his coffee.

Alice hovered her hands over the keyboard.

'You are aware that your business contains part of my business?'

Kosta's eyes narrowed. 'I bought Petó from you and your brother many years ago. Whatever claim you had to it transferred to me on that day.'

From where Alice was sitting, she had a full view of the table. She saw the way Thanos moved his hand to beneath the table, and the way he squeezed his fist so tight his knuckles glowed white.

'But you must dispose of your business,' Thanos said slowly, carefully, with no hint of emotion in the words.

'Why must I?'

'Because you are not married, you have no children, no grandchildren, and because P & A is a family company. You will not list it publicly, nor would you wish it to be broken up and sold off after your death.'

Alice bit down on her lip, sympathy for the older man rushing through her. How strange it must be to have someone refer to your mortality in such a cavalier fashion!

'The fate of my company is not your concern.'

Thanos's eyes narrowed and Alice's heart gave a little lurch. As handsome as he was at any time, like this—formidable and businesslike—he was impossibly fascinating.

Thanos held Kosta's gaze for a long moment, a muscle jerking in his jaw that only Alice was in a position to see. 'Your profit has been down these past two years.'

'It's a tough economy.'

'No, it isn't,' Thanos pushed ruthlessly. 'You're losing market share and you don't know how to get it back.'

Kosta's eyes glinted. 'You think I came here to be lectured?'

Thanos didn't apologise, nor did he back down. 'I'm not telling you anything you don't already know. If you do not act now, your once great business will fade away into insignificance. Thousands of people will lose their jobs. All because you are too stubborn to see what you must do.'

Kosta's rejection of that assertion was obvious. '*My* business. *My* problem.'

At this, Thanos straightened in his chair, his expression like flint. 'I might have agreed to sell Petó to you, but I never stopped thinking of it as mine. You rolled it into your business, which means I care about your business too. Sell me P & A and I will ensure your legacy is safe.'

Kosta let out a laugh of disbelief that had Alice slipping her gaze to focus on the older man's face. 'You think I would trust you with my company?'

'Why should you not?' It was a banal enough question, but Alice heard the undertone of steel and looked to Thanos once more. A tight smile was cracking his face but waves of anger were shifting off his frame.

'Because you are your father's son, and I will not have my family's legacy dragged through the mud.'

Alice sucked in a sharp breath, surprised at how offended she was by the scathing indictment. Thanos turned to face her, the noise apparently drawing his attention, and when their eyes locked, sympathy exploded inside her.

'I know you are not like him,' Kosta hastened to add, an apology inherent in the words. 'You are different. But the potential for scandal is the same.'

Thanos dipped his head forward, so Alice couldn't see how he reacted to this explanation.

'I cannot open my paper without seeing your

photo,' Kosta continued. 'You drink too much, party too much, sleep with any woman who moves. Your reputation as the playboy prince of Europe is almost too mild for your excessive lifestyle.'

Thanos lifted his head, his face like a mask of iron. 'And what is my lifestyle to do with this? Do you think it affects my ability to run your company?'

'I think there is no one better than you,' Kosta contradicted. 'You have a head for business that I have always admired. Even when you were still a boy, following after your grandfather, watching him as though he were an idol brought to life, you had more nous than he and I in our little fingers.'

Alice wondered if Thanos felt pride then, if the compliment did anything to soften his response.

'I learned from the best,' Thanos conceded, finally.

'Yes. Nicholas was one of the best men I have ever known.' Kosta leaned forward, bracing his elbows on the table. 'I always respected him. Liked him. What your father did—'

That same muscle twisted in Thanos's cheek as he ground his teeth together. 'Is not relevant. I made my peace with it a long time ago.'

'Did you?' Kosta's look showed disbelief, but he didn't pursue that line of questioning. He sipped his coffee.

'Your grandfather and I were from a different generation. Things were different. Our parents, and us, we valued family. Old-fashioned morals. We liked things to be respectable. A handshake was as good as a contract.' Kosta shook his head and Alice saw a spark of longing in his eyes. 'The world is different now. Perhaps I am a relic, with no place in it.' His eyes narrowed. 'But if you think I'm going to see my company fall into the hands of a man who regards womanising as a sport, then you know nothing about what this business means.'

Thanos held Kosta's gaze across the table. Neither man faltered and Alice felt as if she was intruding on a deeply personal moment.

'No one will work harder for P & A than I will,' Thanos promised, at length.

'That may be so,' Kosta agreed. 'But I will not sell it to you.'

Alice swept her eyes shut for a moment, more invested in the outcome of this meeting than she would have thought possible.

'I don't intend to take no for an answer.'

'You don't like to hear no from anyone. It's part of why you've been so successful in repairing the damage your father did. But that does not change my answer. I will not sell P & A to a man like you, Thanos Stathakis. Not for twice what you're offering; not for anything. Not until you've grown up.'

* * *

Alice flicked through the pile of bills, a half-eaten sandwich to her left. Her credit card had very little available cash on it—it wouldn't come close to paying off her mother's latest hospitalisation.

Her heart squeezed as she remembered the sight of her mother being rushed through the corridors, the blood clot threatening her life, panic surging through Alice as she knew how close they were to the end.

But Jane Smart had defied all odds and survived—she remained in a coma, but she remained.

Alice flipped over to another bill, nausea filling her. It was too much. How could she ever manage to cover this?

She was so engrossed in her finances that she didn't hear the door to Thanos's office click open, nor did she hear his approach until he was practically on top of her.

Self-consciously, she laid her hand over the bills, aware that it barely covered the bright red paper demanding immediate payment.

'Did you need something, sir?'

He didn't correct her use of the formal title now. He was brooding. Thinking. Even more determined since Kosta had walked out of the office. 'What did you think of Kosta Carinedes?'

Alice was surprised by the question. She sat

back in her chair a little, momentarily forgetting about her bills, and her lunch. 'In what way?'

'In any way. Did you perceive he was serious in his reasons for not wanting to sell to me?'

Alice captured her lower lip with her teeth, gnawing on it thoughtfully. 'I can't see why he would lie,' she said finally.

'No, nor can I. After all, the price I've offered is above the market rate of the company. He's a fool to walk away from it.'

'Perhaps he doesn't really want to sell?'

'He knows he must.' He shook his head, dragging a hand through his hair, throwing it into even greater disarray. 'He's just being stubborn.'

Alice nodded, turning back to her desk thoughtfully. After all, the older man had raised a valid point. Thanos had a reputation for seducing women left, right and centre. He was rarely without a date on his arm, and it didn't seem to be the same woman for long. He partied non-stop, but what did that matter? Everything he touched in a commercial sense turned to gold. Surely that was more important when it came to handing a business over?

'Maybe he'll change his mind,' she offered, lifting her gaze back to his face. He was staring out of the window, his expression unreadable.

'I don't think so.'

'Then you'll just have to change it for him,' she said quietly, turning back to the bills, flicking to the next one with a frown on her face, unaware of the way his eyes swivelled to follow her.

Thanos regarded this mild-mannered assistant thoughtfully. She was plain-spoken and unaffected. Unlike most of the women he dealt with, she wasn't going out of her way to flatter and please him. She was acting as though she barely noticed he was a man. It was unusual for him to come across a woman who didn't respond in a certain way.

And it was fascinating.

She was pretty, he supposed, in an understated way—though she also went to very little effort with her appearance. Her suit was old and boxy, hiding any curves she might have beneath too much fabric. Her hair was silky and luscious, long, he suspected, though it was impossible to know as she wore it pinned in a sensible, low bun at the nape of her neck. In fact, everything about her was sensible. Plain. Businesslike.

His eyes dropped lower, to hands that were sorting through a pile of papers—red, with *OVERDUE* marked at the top. And despite his own monumental problems, curiosity lifted inside him.

'What are you doing?' he asked.

She looked at him with a slight frown on her face, almost as though she thought he might have left.

'I'm catching up on some personal business. It's my lunch break.'

He looked at his watch. 'It's the end of the day.'

'I didn't have time to have it any earlier.' She said it as though she was worried he might be cross with her, as if she feared recriminations. That was unnecessary. Though she was only a temp, and he hadn't been to the New York office for almost a year, Thanos knew that Alice worked harder than most of the permanent executive support team. Her security card was frequently the last one swiped out at the end of the evening, and oftentimes the first one to appear on the staff list.

She worked long hours and, though his workload was nothing if not exhausting, she'd somehow managed to keep his business and personal life running like a well-oiled machine.

If he needed his jet fuelled up, he emailed Alice. Gifts organised, Alice. Anything done with his apartments? Alice. She oversaw all aspects of his life and yet they were only today meeting for the first time.

And he knew nothing about her.

Why did that bother him? He couldn't have said. Stathakis Corp employed thirty thousand people globally. One woman shouldn't have interested him like this.

And yet, he found himself propping his hip on the edge of her desk, and looking at the bills with more interest. She shuffled them self-consciously.

So he knew one thing about her.

She was a poor money manager. She had to be, given what the temp rates were for an executive assistant at this level. Sure, there was agency commission to come out of her salary packet, but regardless of that, her rate was generous.

'Did you need anything else, sir?'

She spoke without looking at him, but he detected a faint tremble in her fingertips as she filed the bills under some other papers, pointedly reaching for her sandwich.

He straightened, with a frown. 'No.' As he moved towards the door, his frown didn't ease.

'How long do you expect to be in New York?'

Her question caught him off-guard. Thanos never liked to be anywhere for long. He'd arrived in Manhattan a day earlier anticipating his business here would be wrapped up within twenty-four hours. Now he paused, with no idea when he'd be able to get out of town.

'I have no idea.'

Silence for a moment and then, 'So I'll see you tomorrow?'

He turned back to face her, and there was no

warmth in her expression. In fact, he couldn't have said if she'd asked the question with curiosity or apprehension, but both sparked a ridiculous urge to laugh.

Instead, he nodded stiffly. 'Yes. Goodnight, Alice.'

CHAPTER TWO

'WHAT YOU NEED is to get married, Thanos.'

Leonidas's words came to Thanos as if through a thousand galaxies—crackly and distant. He jerked out of bed, completely naked, and strode through his penthouse apartment.

His brother's statement was exploding through his brain, like stardust and gold. He reached for the crystal decanter of Scotch and poured himself a generous measure, moving towards the grand piano and tapping a key lightly. Manhattan glistened beneath him, all shimmering lights and elaborate dreams.

This was the first time in years he'd been alone in this city. Usually, he called one of his past lovers—of which there were many here in the city—and enjoyed a night of unbridled, no-strings passion.

But the meeting with Kosta had left him inexplicably dissatisfied.

Thanos was a master at keeping his personal life separate from his private life. The fact he had a well-documented and active bachelor lifestyle was neither here nor there. He knew he was, un-equivocally, the right person to take over P & A.

And beyond that, Petó deserved to come home.

'I know it's out of left field but have you actually passed out?' Leonidas's words were filled with humour.

Thanos sipped his Scotch slowly, his eyes moving from one high rise to another. When he eventually spoke, it was with a sardonic drawl. 'I understand that you're in the heady bliss of being a newly-wed but I think we can safely say marriage is the last thing on my mind.' In fact, the very idea turned his blood cold. One week after his mother had dumped him on Dion Stathakis's doorstep, throwing a traumatised little boy into the home as one might a cat into a flock of pigeons, Thanos had sworn to Leonidas that he'd never be stupid enough to fall in love or get married.

He'd been eight and miserable, his heart broken, his soul crushed—looking back, he could see now that he'd also been terrified. His mother, the woman who'd raised him, the only family he'd ever known, had told him she couldn't 'do this' any more, and dropped him like a sack of potatoes.

His father had made it abundantly clear he didn't want Thanos, that he was raising him out of duty. When Dion's own marriage had crumbled because of Thanos's unexpected arrival, a large part of Thanos's heart had been sealed closed—he knew it would never open again.

Was it any wonder Thanos viewed relationships and commitment as something best avoided?

'I don't mean a *real* marriage,' Leonidas explained with mock simplicity.

Beyond the window, dusk was falling, the night sky turning an inky black, no stars to be seen in the brightness cast by the vibrant city. Thanos cradled his drink in the palm of his hand.

'Kosta has given you the solution; you're just not listening. He won't accept any offer you make because you're a walking tabloid headline. This isn't just a top five hundred company he's selling. It's his *family* empire.'

'It's *our* family empire too.'

'He bought Petó a long time ago. I doubt he continues to consider it as a distinct entity from P & A.'

'And nor do I. I am not attempting to separate Petó from the fold. I am willing to take on his business as well.'

'Yes, I get that. But he's not willing to sell to us. Not given your…predilection for headline-grabbing behaviour.'

Thanos stiffened, the criticism sitting uneasily around his shoulders now. He'd never felt uncomfortable about his lifestyle before; he'd never had any reason to. But hearing first Kosta and then his brother cast aspersions on the way he lived was filling Thanos with a sense of impatience. 'My social life is no impediment to my running Stathakis,' he heard himself point out coldly.

'True, but neither of us could do anything worse than our father did to trash our family name, right?'

Thanos winced, sympathy for his brother at the forefront of his mind. Years had passed since that awful day when Leonidas's young family had been murdered as a vendetta against their father but even now that Leonidas was married with a beautiful little girl who was growing *way* too fast, Thanos still felt sorrow for what had been lost.

'You and I are nothing like our father.'

'I know.' Leonidas and Thanos were quiet for a moment, their point of difference from Dion Stathakis one of sheer determination. Both men had sworn, many years earlier, even before his criminal prosecution, that they would never emulate his lifestyle. They had always admired their grandfather and followed much more closely in Nicholas's footsteps.

'So show Kosta he's wrong about you,' Leonidas continued, his voice insistent. 'He thinks you're just some debauched tycoon, with more money and sex appeal than sense—'

'So? Even if that were accurate—' and he didn't want to contemplate how many threads of truth there were to that observation '—I'm the best man to turn that company around and make sure it continues to thrive in the twenty-first century. No one will care for the business as I will; you know that.'

'Yes,' Leonidas conceded softly.

'So what? Because I happen to like sex and the tabloids happen to like me, he thinks I'm not qualified?'

'He wants more than just a business deal,' Leonidas said gently. 'The company's his legacy. It's not just a business to him—it's a way of life, and it's his birthright. He wants to protect that.'

Thanos had no difficulties relating to Kosta's desires on that score. His own life had been devoid of the kind of parents most people grew up with. His mother had abandoned him and his father had taken him in reluctantly, but there had been grandparents and what wouldn't Thanos have done for them? What wouldn't he have done in their honour?

Wasn't it because of them that Leonidas and Thanos had worked tirelessly for the better part of a decade to restore Stathakis Corp to the behemoth it had been before their father's fall from grace? To restore, in part, the Stathakis name?

And wasn't it largely what drove him now?

A desire to bring home Petó, an important and missing piece of the puzzle that was their empire? They'd diversified in their restructure, buying up tech companies, new economy investments to shore up the old. But still, he'd never forgotten the promise he'd made to himself on the day they'd signed the contracts. He had hated selling Petó, the transport company his grandfather had been so proud of, the company that had enabled all their later successes. It meant *everything* to Thanos, and clearly it meant everything to Kosta.

So Thanos just had to show Kosta that the legacy was safe in his hands.

If only Kosta could see that the best way to preserve what his grandparents had built was to sell the company to a man who would have the skills, acumen and motivation to take the whole enterprise to the next level.

'You are a fool if you don't simply tick this box for Kosta and move on. Get married and he will sell it to you in an instant.'

Thanos threw his Scotch back, his brother's suggestion making an infuriating kind of sense, despite his determination never to marry.

'Putting aside for the moment the fact that he's going to see through this play in an instant, who would I even marry if I were to go through with it?'

Leonidas laughed. 'There must be hundreds

of women you've slept with. Choose the one you like the best.'

'I don't like any of them enough to marry. And I don't generally go back for repeat performances.'

Leonidas's sigh came down the phone line. 'If you want the company, you're going to have to make your peace with this. It's the only way.'

'It's crazy.'

'No, it's actually very sensible.'

'I cannot simply marry some random woman.'

'Why not?'

'Because I'd be doing it purely for commercial gain.'

'So? Find someone who would be marrying you for their own commercial gain. Or have you forgotten what you're worth?'

'It's completely unscrupulous.'

'Why?'

'To fake a marriage to fool an old man?'

Leonidas was quiet a moment. 'Do you not think the end justifies the means?'

Thanos ground his teeth together. He could accept many things in life, but not losing Petó.

Besides, Leonidas was right—Kosta had all but drawn a map for Thanos as to how he could succeed in the purchase.

Settle down. Stop being so wild. At least appear to have become a family man.

So perhaps his brother had a point.

Marriage.

He might hate the idea of getting married, but a wedding like this—with each partner knowing it was purely mercenary? If he was clear on that point from the outset?

If there was an escape route always within reach?

So that no matter what happened he would know there was a definite termination point established, a date when the marriage would end and his life could go back to normal?

Perhaps that kind of marriage wouldn't be so bad. A marriage, in name only. But to whom?

Alice disconnected the call with wobbly fingers and stared at her office wall. Tears that she rarely allowed herself to give into cloyed at her throat, so she had to press the heel of her palm to her eyes to stop from crying.

Bankruptcy.

The word hung in the air like a thousand little arrows, pointed at her soul. How could it have come to this? No matter how hard she worked, she could never get ahead, and now her credit-card company was demanding she close her accounts, settling her debts in full, or they'd commence bankruptcy proceedings.

She clamped her teeth down on her lip, trying to stave off an actual sob, trying to see some kind of light, somewhere, at the end of this tunnel. There had to be something she could sell, something she could do.

Except, there wasn't. She'd hawked everything of value over the years, reluctantly parting with anything they could make money from, including the diamond earrings her mother had loved so much—a gift from Alice's father, when they'd first met.

She hadn't been able to go to college, she couldn't get a job that paid more than this one, and no reputable bank would touch her with a barge pole in terms of a loan. She knew what her credit rating was.

She let out a guttural noise of impatience and stood, pacing across the office, nausea tightening her stomach. There had to be *something*.

A single tear slid from one of her eyes, rolling down her cheek, and at that exact moment Thanos Stathakis appeared in the door frame of his office, looking out at her, his expression as forbidding and handsome as it had been the day before.

He opened his mouth to speak, then saw her expression and closed it. His eyes roamed her face quite freely, and Alice stood completely still, so overwhelmed that she didn't even think to wipe away her tear.

'Did you need something?' Her voice was a little wobbly, but there was pride in her question, because she wasn't going to let things get any worse by acting unprofessionally.

His lips tugged downwards at the corner. 'Yes. Come in.' He waved a hand in the direction of his office and Alice sucked in a breath, moving quickly to her desk and sliding her credit-card statement under her keyboard before doing as he'd said and stepping into his massive workspace.

'Please, have a seat.' He gestured to the boardroom table.

She shook her head. Alice didn't feel like sitting down.

'You're upset?'

She blinked, shaking her head, lifting her fingers to her cheeks now and wiping her tears. 'No,' she lied—badly. 'I'm fine. What did you need?'

His eyes narrowed but he turned away from her, apparently accepting her statement, pouring a cool glass of water and carrying it across the room. When he passed it to her, their fingers brushed and a jolt of electricity travelled the length of Alice's arm, burning brightly into her chest cavity.

'You may feel better if you speak about what is troubling you,' he invited.

Alice's eyes flew wide, this kindness completely unexpected. 'I… It's my problem,' she demurred.

Thanos nodded slowly, assimilating this information. 'And you like to solve your problems yourself,' he surmised.

Alice nodded. 'As, I think, do you.'

His smile lacked humour; in fact, his smile had the look of someone who'd almost forgotten how. 'Wherever possible, certainly.' He crossed his arms over his broad chest, a gesture that drew her attention to his muscled abdomen in a way that sparked heat in her cheeks.

'But you're inviting me to pour my heart out to you?' she prompted, to which he pulled a face, as if it was actually the last thing he'd been expecting. Alice laughed, despite her enormous worries.

'I'm saying… I don't like tears.' The words were uneasy. 'If talking would help…'

Her heart lurched a little inside her chest. Alice didn't want to think about how long it had been since she'd had anyone she could speak to. It felt like an eternity.

'It's hard to explain,' she said, sipping the water with hands that were still unsteady.

He was quiet. Watchful. Some might have said calculating, but Alice didn't know Thanos well enough to see that glint in his eye, nor was she looking for it. She paced towards the boardroom table, placing her water down, her eyes focussed on the stunning view of Manhattan. Somehow, it was easier to speak without looking at him.

'It's my mom,' she said, shaking her head, because that wasn't, strictly speaking, the truth. 'I mean, it is and it isn't. She's…not well. And looking after her is hard, and expensive, and it's been years now, and no matter what I do, I can't seem to get on top of it, and I have no idea what to do or how I can make this any easier.' She ground her teeth together, but it didn't help; a sob bubbled up and out of her chest. She looked at him apologetically. 'I'm never like this at work, I swear.'

'I know that.' His voice was carefully blanked of emotion.

'I mean, I work really hard, because I can't risk getting a bad reference, because I need the next job, and at the moment I'm one of the top-rated temps at the agency, so I work hard to make sure I don't lose that.'

Thanos considered this. 'Would permanent employment not suit you better? You'd get a steadier salary.'

'True.' Alice nodded. 'But the pay is way less, and I need some flexibility. There are times when I have to be off work for two or three weeks to help with mom, and if I'm a temp, that's a lot easier to arrange.'

'So you support your mother?'

'Yes.' She nodded. 'She had a stroke. She's in a coma. I can't afford a bed in a home so she lives with me, and the cost of home nursing—which she needs through the day—is astronomical. I'm basically working to cover her medical bills and then there's food and rent and...' A tear slid down her cheek. 'I'm sorry.'

'What for?' He surprised her then, pulling a tissue from the drawer of his desk and striding across to her. Instead of handing the tissue to her, he dabbed at her cheeks. It was a gesture of such kindness that it somehow made her feel worse, rather than better.

She wasn't used to anyone helping her. Listening to her. And it was as if a crack had formed into which she wanted to pour all her grief, all her worries. But he was her boss, and this was a job, and she'd already created a bad enough impression without making it worse.

'Thank you.' She spoke firmly, taking a step back, away from him, away from sympathy. 'I don't know what came over me. It's just been one of those days.'

She lifted the water glass from the table, intending to take it to the kitchen to wash it, but he put a hand on her wrist, stilling her. Only it didn't still *all* of her. Alice's blood thundered at the light, innocent touch.

'I also have a problem, Alice,' he said, his

eyes boring into hers with an intensity that sent a shiver down her spine. It was easy to see in that moment how he had, side by side with his brother, turned a crumbling business into a global behemoth. She felt strength slamming into her from every single pore of his body.

But his words didn't quite make sense. Did he wish to unburden himself? Did he want a sympathetic ear? It didn't exactly fit with the character profile she had of Thanos but Alice found herself listening intently.

'And it occurs to me that we could be of use to one another.'

Her eyes flared wide at this idea. Without knowing any details, she knew she shouldn't get her hopes up. And yet, it felt like…a light in the dark.

'How so?'

'My brother suggested last night that I should give Kosta Carinedes exactly what he wants.'

'You're going to stop getting photographed by paparazzi?' Alice prompted, a hint of scepticism in her words, because the media loved Thanos and his antics like bees loved nectar.

'I'm not sure that's possible.' He echoed her unspoken doubts. 'But I'm going to give them the right thing to photograph.'

'What do you mean?'

'If Kosta wants me to settle down, then I'll do just that. I'll get married.'

It was so absurd that Alice laughed. 'You're getting married?'

'That depends.'

'On…?'

'On if you'll agree to be my wife.'

CHAPTER THREE

'DON'T THINK OF it as a marriage,' he added, when she hadn't spoken for several long, confused seconds of silence. 'Think of it as a job offer.'

'To be your wife?' She roused herself, finally, blinking as though that might help make sense of matters.

Thanos's eyes narrowed speculatively. 'Yes.'

'Do you feel okay? Are you drunk?'

He laughed; a hoarse sound. 'No.'

'You can't seriously be expecting me to marry you?'

'Why not?'

'Um…' She sipped her water for something to do. 'Because we just met yesterday?'

'Yes,' he agreed. 'But I already know everything I need to know to make this marriage a success.'

Alice lifted her brows in a silent entreaty for him to continue.

'You are efficient, trustworthy and intelligent. I have been very impressed with your work ethic.'

Pleasure zipped through her.

'But more than that, Alice, you need money, and this marriage would simply be a business arrangement.'

'A business arrangement?' She echoed his pronouncement, trying to make sense of that.

'Why not?'

A crease formed between her brows and she lifted a hand, tucking a loose bit of chestnut hair behind her ear. 'Is that even legal?'

His smile held a hint of derision. 'You think arranged marriages are not binding?'

'I...' She couldn't think straight. 'I'm sorry. This has come totally out of the blue. You're seriously saying you want to marry me?'

His gaze was laced with fierce determination, sharp enough to send a blade of apprehension down her spine. 'I would do anything to get Petó back. Kosta has made his terms clear. This is the only way to fulfil them.'

'I can kind of see that, I guess.' She sounded anything but convinced. 'Except I'm the last woman you'd ever marry. He's never going to believe this is genuine.'

'On the contrary, the fact that you are not like the kind of women I am attracted to makes you perfect for this ruse.'

Alice let out a soft laugh, hiding the way his pronouncement hurt. She knew she wasn't particularly beautiful, and she had no hope that a man like Thanos would ever look twice at her. Not that she wanted him to—she was done with men, done with love altogether. Still, she had a little pride left and in that moment it had been completely hollowed out. 'How do you figure?'

'Because you *are* different. It makes sense that when I do eventually settle down, it would be with someone who challenges me, who stands out compared to my usual…type.'

She resisted the urge to pull a face, even though this conversation was becoming some-what mortifying. 'Okay, fair enough. But we just met yesterday.'

'He doesn't know that.'

'I…'

'For all he knows, you and I have been seeing one another for months.'

Alice lifted a brow. 'Well, that would hardly be a ringing endorsement of my judgement.' She lifted her hands apologetically, but con-tinued explaining. 'I mean, you've been in the papers—recently—photographed with differ-ent women.'

He waved a hand in the air, as though it barely mattered. 'Kosta is an intelligent man, who has also done his share of living in the public eye. He knows as well as I do that papers make stuff up. I don't particularly care what is written about me. I understand the newspapers and blogs have a job to do, but only a fool would take gossip as gospel.'

Alice ignored the implication that she was a fool, given that it had never occurred to her to question what was written about him. 'I just can't see this working.'

Determination fired in Thanos's expression. 'I would not suggest it if I didn't think we could convince Kosta.'

Alice's stomach flipped and flopped. 'Marriage is a very permanent way to fix a problem like this.'

His smile was bordering on indulgent and Alice felt, suddenly, very naïve. 'Marriages frequently end in divorce; ours would be just the same.'

'Fated from the beginning,' she said, nodding slowly.

'As most are.'

She was too caught up in the complexity of this to properly note the hard cynicism to his voice.

'So how would it work?'

He expelled a breath, as though he was relieved, taking her acquiescence for granted, so she hastened to add, 'I'm not saying yes. I'm just curious as to the details.'

'I admire your prudence.'

More pleasure, this time slamming against her ribs and catching her completely unawares. 'Have you eaten lunch?'

'Lunch?' The unexpected question roused her from her thoughts. She thought of the bare pantry at home, and her stomach grumbled betrayingly. 'No.'

'Fine. Let's go and discuss this properly.'

'It's two o'clock in the afternoon.'

'So?' He gestured towards the door with his natural authority and she found herself walking towards it.

But as she crossed the threshold, she felt the need to insist, 'I'm not agreeing to this, Thanos. I think this is one of the craziest ideas I've ever heard, actually.'

'Fine.' He nodded, brushing aside her objection with ease. 'But you are intrigued, no?'

'Yes,' she admitted, a half-smile reluctantly lifting her lips. 'I'm intrigued.'

'Good.' He grinned. 'Then this is a beginning.' He moved to the elevator, pressing the button. It opened instantly. 'I promise, I will make it impossible for you to refuse me, Alice.'

She stepped into the lift, and when it began to ascend instead of descend, she suspected the loopy feeling in her tummy had very little to do with the sudden change in altitude.

Alice knew there was a helipad on the roof of

the building. She didn't know that a helicopter was parked there, nor that it was sleek and black, the sky equivalent of a private limousine. As they walked towards it, Thanos pressed something in his pocket and the door slid open.

'After you,' he prompted, as if all of this was completely normal. Alice stared at the aircraft, her mouth open in sheer awe, but after a few seconds she pulled it together, forced herself to take a breath and step up into the helicopter's interior. It was like nothing she'd ever seen before. All beige caramel and white glossy wood, pure luxury and glamour.

Thanos took the seat beside her, and, despite the generous proportions of the craft, he made it feel tiny. She was conscious of his every exhalation, conscious of the way his frame was so large that his legs were so, so close to touching hers. She kept her own pinned together, her hands in her lap.

'Clip in,' he said, turning to face her, nodding towards the seat belt.

Alice reached behind her, fumbling the seat belt as she tried to clip it into the unfamiliar lock. He reached over, his eyes holding hers, a slight smile at the edges of his face. 'May I?'

Feeling both naïve and stupid, she nodded. 'Thank you.' The words were crisp, and she was glad she'd spoken before he actually reached for the seat belt. Because the way he dragged it across her body sent a thousand volts of electricity into her nervous system, so heat pooled in her gut and spread through her limbs.

It was an innocent gesture though, and Alice had to remind herself that she was definitely not his type. That was the reason he was proposing this ridiculous marriage of convenience. Except—was it really so ridiculous? She could perfectly see the benefit to him, if it meant he could secure the purchase of P & A.

And for Alice?

Dared she hope he would offer some kind of salary to her—better than she was earning now—in order for her to go along with this? That had to be what he had in mind.

'Here.' He handed her a white headset then looped his own in place, before flicking some dials and switches and bringing the rotor blades to life. The noise was loud—too loud to speak over. He tapped the headset again, smiling as he lifted up off the rooftop.

'Where are we going?' she yelled, despite the fact she had a small microphone hooked up to the headset, so he winced a little, sending her a look of amusement.

'Sorry.' She laughed. 'Where are we going?' A whisper now.

Then he laughed, and the sound was like sun-warmed caramel, her body warmed in an instant and involuntary response.

'Lunch.'

She arched a brow. 'I thought you meant a sandwich at the deli downstairs.'

It was his turn to pull a face, his expression scandalised. 'That's not food.'

'It's…not?'

'I do not like this American way of eating while you are doing other things. Sandwiches!' He said the word as if it was an affront to good food everywhere, and she found a small smile playing about her lips.

'Sandwiches are actually very practical. Portable, tasty, filling…'

He shrugged. 'Boring.'

And she understood then, because Thanos enjoyed nice things. He enjoyed experiences. Parties. Food. Wine. The sun on his body as he sunned himself on the deck of his yacht.

'You're a hedonist.'

He turned to face her. 'Perhaps. But shouldn't we all be?'

Alice didn't say anything. She didn't want to remind Thanos that she'd spent the better part of the last few years wondering how long she could survive on just potatoes, or just bread.

'So where are we going?'

'A little place I know.'

The 'little place he knew' turned out to be a restaurant in Brooklyn, so exclusive it wasn't even signposted. He brought his helicopter down on the roof of a building that was only about ten stories tall, busying himself with the technical requirements of flying for a few moments. Moments in which Alice sat completely still and tried to get her head around this bizarre turn of events.

It only became more bizarre when they entered the restaurant through the kitchen and the chefs stopped what they were doing to basically fawn over Thanos. They all wanted to speak to him, and, to his credit, he took a moment with each of them, and seemed to know most of their names. She watched, fascinated, as he asked questions of each, managing small details—the names of their children or partners, offering condolences to one woman who, Alice gathered, had recently lost her father.

'You come here often?' she prompted as they swept into the restaurant itself—a loft space that could have accommodated a hundred diners but which had instead been converted into a room that felt almost like a penthouse lounge, all elegant sofas interspersed with enormous fiddle-leaf fig plants in copper pots. This made it possible for the dining tables to be set far apart, creating complete privacy, and suddenly Alice understood the appeal.

No one would hear their conversation; they could speak entirely unobserved.

He held a chair out for her only seconds before a waiter appeared.

'Mr Stathakis, welcome back. Would you like to see a menu?'

Thanos tilted his head towards Alice. 'I usually just eat what is served. However, you might like to take a look?'

'No, that's fine.' She shook her head. 'Whatever you have will be great, I'm sure.'

'I can ask if they will serve you sandwiches?' he teased and her heart skipped a beat.

'That would be lovely.' She winked to show she was joking.

Thanos grinned, dismissing the waiter with a few words in Greek, before taking the seat opposite her. She felt an unwelcome burst of nerves, and did her best to quell them.

In the office, his proposition had been surprising. On the helicopter, she'd been overawed by the glamour and completely unusual turn of events. But here, in a romantic, secluded restaurant, sitting across from one of the world's wealthiest men—to say nothing of his personal charms and physical appeal—Alice's pulse was trembling unstoppably.

'Relax,' he murmured, apparently intuiting her panic.

'I'm sorry, it's just not every day I get proposed to,' she said with a sardonic smile.

'But this is not a real proposal,' he reminded her smoothly, his eyes intent on hers. 'It is a business proposition.'

'You'd know more about that than I do.'

He nodded. 'Let me explain it for you,' he offered. 'Just like in business, we would have a contract to protect both of our interests.'

'A pre-nuptial agreement?'

'A divorce settlement,' he corrected. 'I would have our divorce papers confidentially drawn up and filed by my personal lawyer, on terms we will agree to now.'

'What kind of terms?' she asked quickly, her heart racing.

He examined her thoughtfully, then shrugged. 'What would you like?'

Alice's stomach swooped to her toes. 'You want me to choose?'

'In a negotiation, it is normal for one party to come in with a list of demands. You know what I need from you, so tell me, Alice, what do you need from me?'

She chewed on her lip, the possibilities endless. 'I want not to worry about my mom,' she said, simply. 'She needs to be in a home. A good one. Somewhere with kind staff where she can be as…

comfortable as possible.' Alice's voice cracked. 'Somewhere I can go and see her often.'

Thanos nodded. 'Fine. What else?'

It was on the tip of Alice's tongue to say that was everything she needed, but when she thought of her overburdened credit cards, the threatened bankruptcy, she decided she might as well go for broke. 'I'd need to continue earning my temp salary,' she said, tilting her chin to show she was serious. 'I presume in order to make this seem legitimate, I wouldn't be able to work, but I'd need to continue earning so I could cover rent for as long as we were married. That way, I'll have my apartment to come back to,' she tacked on, when he didn't speak.

He remained silent, staring at her for so long and so hard that she wondered if she'd pushed it too far.

And then he laughed, a cracking sound that reverberated around the room.

'What?' Heat spread through her cheeks.

'Your old apartment? *Dio*, Alice.' He shook his head, laughter lines still creasing the corners of his eyes. 'I can see that of your many strengths, negotiating is not one of them.'

Her heart rate notched up a gear. She knew the cost of a bed in a good nursing home wasn't cheap. It would be half a million dollars, easily, to buy an ongoing position.

'So tell me what you want to pay me,' she said instead.

'I am asking you to walk away from your life, to pretend to be my wife—which is not likely to be a walk in the park, let me tell you. You would be photographed, and I would expect you to attend events with me often, in order to sell this as real. You will need to completely overhaul your way of life. And you ask for only your salary?'

Her jaw dropped. 'And my mother's care.'

He waved a hand in the air, dismissively.

'I wasn't sure what you had in mind.'

'Alice, you should not undervalue yourself like this.'

'Well, what do *you* suggest?'

'For starters, an apartment in New York. You can choose what you like. I have several, but if none of them is to your liking then feel free to contact a realtor.'

Her jaw dropped lower.

'A cash settlement. I was expecting you to ask for twenty million dollars, to which I intended to counter ten, and settle on perhaps fifteen after some back and forth. So shall we just save ourselves the trouble and say fifteen million dollars?'

'Fifteen million dollars? In cash?'

'Alice, I'm a very wealthy man, and if you marry me, you'll be enabling me to buy a business that is worth more to me than anything else. *Yes.* Fifteen million dollars.'

'And a home in New York. And my mother's care.'

'And health insurance,' he seemed to add as an afterthought. 'Starting immediately.'

Alice gaped. It was too much.

'But I could just pay for that myself with the money…'

He laughed again. 'Your negotiation skills are really quite poor.'

'I don't want to feel like I'm scamming you.'

Surprise crossed his face, but he covered it quickly. 'You're not.'

'It feels a lot like I am.'

'It's a job.'

'A ridiculously over-paid job.'

'I'm already paying above the odds for the company.' He shrugged. 'This is just another expense to factor into its reacquisition.'

'It means that much to you?'

His eyes glittered like black gemstones and in response he simply dipped his head forward.

'Petó means everything to me.'

'Because it used to be yours?'

'Because it was my grandfather's.' And despite the fact the words were delivered quietly, she felt passion in every single syllable. 'Because it was sold under duress, and because I swore I

would get it back.' He closed his eyes for a moment. 'And because Kosta Carinedes will sell
eventually, and I do not wish him to sell it to
anyone else.'

'You think he would?'

Thanos pierced her with his gaze. 'Yes.'

'So how would this work?' she prompted,
breaking off when the waiter reappeared with a
bottle of wine. Alice watched as he unscrewed
the cork and poured two glasses, then disappeared once more.

'We'd get married quickly. Two weeks should
be enough time to organise the details. I have
a hotel in the South of France that would be
perfect—just the kind of place I would choose
for my wedding. It's private and difficult to
get to, so while we'll leak it to the press, there
won't be an abundance of paparazzi hanging
off the gates.'

A shiver ran down her spine at the image he
created, and she fought an urge to ask him about
his life—how it felt to be hounded everywhere he
went. She was curious, but there were far more
pressing concerns. 'Two weeks?' The words
came out strangled.

'It has to be soon. The way his figures are
tanking, he's going to become desperate to sell,
and I would not risk him testing the market by
listing his business interests.'

Alice swallowed. That made perfect sense. And yet…it was so soon.

'And your mother could be moved into a suitable facility as early as tomorrow,' he promised, making Alice's stomach twist, because she would do anything for her mother—*anything*—and here Thanos was promising a solution that would finally take away their concerns.

'That's…the wedding,' she heard herself respond stiffly, just a whisper, and her eyes dropped to the table nervously. She reached for her wine glass, lifting it and taking a gulp that did little to settle her frazzled nerves.

He sat opposite, waiting for her to finish, and eventually, Alice lifted her face, staring at him nervously for several anguished beats. 'I'm talking about the marriage.'

The words emerged as barely a croak, so Thanos had to lean forward to hear them better.

'Go on?' he prompted.

Alice's cheeks felt sun-warmed from embarrassment. 'I get that there'll be a big wedding, but what about the marriage?'

'What about it?'

'How long would you envisage this going on for?'

He shrugged. 'A year?'

'A year!' She gulped more wine back.

'We would not have to live together that whole

time,' he back-pedalled. 'Just for the first few months, while I was getting the deal through with Kosta.'

'Live together?' The words squeaked out, her eyes slamming shut in silent refutation of this very idea.

'Well, yes. I mean, that's kind of the point...'

Alice's blood was rushing through her so hard and fast it was all she could hear. She gaped, her lips moving with no sound coming out.

When she finally dared to glance at Thanos, she found him watching her with a concentration that almost robbed her of all breath. 'I can't... I mean... I can't live with you.'

He arched a brow. 'No?'

Her cheeks weren't pink now, they were bright red. 'I'm not... I mean... I know you're very... erm...sophisticated, but I'm not, and I'm not interested in the kind of relationship you're...suggesting.'

He stared at her for several seconds and then burst out laughing, so she frowned, with no idea what he found so laughable.

'Relax, Alice. I'm not propositioning you for sex.'

She felt as if she were about to have a heart attack. Mortification spread through her and she lifted the wine glass once more, drinking at least half of what remained in one quick sip.

It burned all the way down her throat, the unfamiliar flavour like acid. 'You just said we were going to live together.'

'Yes,' he agreed with a shrug. 'But behind closed doors, our relationship will be as it is now. Businesslike. Professional. Courteous. In fact, we probably won't see much of each other, given how much I travel.'

'And you'd continue to travel,' she murmured, her heart rate slowing to something approaching normal.

He nodded. 'I don't see any reason to make huge changes to either of our lives, behind closed doors.'

'But you wouldn't see other women?' she blurted out, wondering why that bothered her so much. Pride, she supposed. Pride, and her experience with Clinton, and having seen what her father was capable of. She didn't want to be used by some man, made a laughing stock. Not again.

'I do not really "see" women now,' he pointed out with a lift of his shoulders.

'But you couldn't be photographed flirting with some supermodel at a party,' she insisted. 'If the whole point is to fool Mr Carinedes, then you'll need to play the part of a doting newly-wed as much as I will.'

'This is not exactly a hardship,' he said with a

dip of his head. 'As you know, I am very motivated to succeed in this.'

'I know,' she whispered, gripping her wineglass stem as though it were a lifeline.

'I spend most of my time in Greece,' he continued, as though this matter were dealt with. 'I presume once I have arranged suitable accommodation for your mother, you will be able to join me there?'

Her mouth dropped open, her tongue darting out to trace the line of her lower lip; she barely noticed the way his eyes fell to the gesture.

'Alice?'

'I...yes.' She nodded, painfully aware of the void that was her private life.

He took a moment to consider that and then smiled, relaxed, relieved. 'So?' He lifted a brow and her heart *kerthunked* hard against her chest in a vicious, imperious warning.

Because only a fool would fail to see the danger here. The danger in agreeing to marry a man like Thanos Stathakis, with more charm and sex appeal in his little finger than any man had a right to possess.

'It would be purely business,' she insisted. 'I wouldn't be marrying you for any reason except to get out of debt. And to help you,' she admitted grudgingly, because it was true.

He nodded. 'And the same could be said for me. Shall we shake on it to seal the deal?'

And while there might have been a thousand and one more traditional and romantic ways to cement a marriage proposal, shaking hands perfectly suited the sensible, commercial nature of this agreement.

Just business, not personal, and for no longer than a year.

Alice could most definitely live with that.

CHAPTER FOUR

'YOU COULD CONSULT with a lawyer,' Thanos offered.

Alice lifted her gaze from the divorce contracts, a look of cool determination in her gaze. For the first time in a long time, she felt as if she was in control of her life, she felt as if things were going to be okay, and she desperately needed to believe that. Already, things were so much better. Two days after her agreeing to marry Thanos, a bed had been made available for Jane Smart at an upscale nursing home, only an hour's drive from Manhattan.

Thanos had flown Alice to inspect the facility in his helicopter, and she'd been completely floored by how perfect everything was. And how considerate he was, in taking her to inspect it himself.

More to the point, it had all been so *easy*. Money, apparently, opened doors, and Thanos had the kind of money that made anything possible. He'd smoothed the way to this marriage completely, paying Alice's rent for a year so she wouldn't feel rushed to move out of her own place, giving her time to think about where to store her things, what she wanted to take with her into her new life.

And now, in his Manhattan penthouse, he was taking the time to meticulously explain the divorce settlement to her.

If only she were able to give it one hundred per cent of her focus!

If only she weren't completely distracted! By the spectacularly expensive apartment—all designer furniture, black leather, polished wood, with high ceilings and glistening chandeliers, and a wrap-around balcony that showed stunning views of Manhattan and Central Park.

And beyond the apartment, there was Thanos.

Dressed casually.

In jeans and a simple T-shirt, he was undeniably handsome, but it was more than that. It was his thoughtfulness, his astuteness, his attention to detail and the rich, husky tone of his voice. She found her pulse throbbing ferociously in her veins as she toyed with the pen, so perhaps he interpreted her actions as hesitation, rather than a desire not to keep staring at his pectoral muscles.

'Do you think I need to see a lawyer?' she threw the question back to him, turning her attention to the papers once more.

'No,' he shook his head once. 'It is as we discussed. But if you doubt my word...'

'I don't.' She couldn't say why, but she trusted him. She smiled distractedly. 'It's just a big thing to do, you know.'

'Yes.' He reached over and curved his hand over hers, so heat spun through Alice. 'But it is just make-believe, and this contract proves that you have a way out.'

She nodded. 'I know.'

'At any point, either of us can file these papers and commence divorce proceedings.' His smile barely changed his expression. 'Think of it as an insurance policy.'

She nodded, lifting her hand and running it through her dark hair. It was pulled back in a bun, but suddenly her head ached and she needed to release the tension pain. She pulled the pins out on autopilot, as she did every evening, slipping them into the pocket of her battered leather handbag—which was completely incongruous with this designer space—before running her fingers through the long, dark waves. Her eyes remained on the divorce papers.

It was all exactly as he'd said on the day he'd proposed.

She skimmed the clauses, reassuring herself with growing disbelief of the amount he'd offered, and the property value cap—which was frankly exorbitant!—in the instance that none of his apartments suited her, and finally hovered the pen over the signature line at the bottom.

Her eyes lifted to his and, with the sense that she was stepping over the edge of the cliff, she added her signature.

Thanos expelled a long, steady breath, then stood up from his chair, coming to stand behind Alice and leaning forward so he could add his own signature to the papers. Only, the action brought his powerful frame so close to hers, he was almost wrapped around her, and suddenly her blood was pounding even harder and faster, making any kind of thought impossible. She swallowed to bring moisture back to her instantly dry throat.

'So, that's it?' she murmured, her eyes scanning his.

'Almost.'

'What else is there?'

He reached into his pocket, pulling out a black velvet box with a world-renowned jeweller's name emblazoned across the top in gold writing.

Alice looked at the box without making an effort to touch it.

'Your ring,' he prompted after a beat.

Only then did Alice slowly push her hand across the table, her fingers trembling as she cracked open the lid.

She couldn't have said what she'd expected. Certainly something worthy of the bride of Thanos Stathakis. But this?

It was ludicrous. She lifted the solitaire ring from its velvet enclosure. Without any real experience it was impossible for Alice to say if the diamond was ten carats or twenty, only that it was as large as two of her thumb nails put together, and so bright it almost blinded her. The setting was simple, six claws and platinum gold.

She felt Thanos's eyes on her as she slid it onto her finger, the weight of it strangely familiar, something she felt she could get used to.

'It's...lovely.' She swallowed past a sudden lump in her throat.

Thanos shrugged. 'I thought it appropriate.'

'It is.' She looked up at him, a small frown tweaking her lips. 'Is this what the women you date would generally expect?'

'A ring like that?' He lifted his shoulders once more. 'I suppose so.'

She shook her head. 'Not just the ring. The whole deal.' Her hand gestured towards the divorce settlement. Thanos's eyes followed the gesture.

'No, *agape*. If this were a real marriage, my wife would undoubtedly expect a lot more.'

Shock was reflected in Alice's expression. 'Seriously?'

'You know what I'm worth?'

Alice tilted her head to the side. 'A lot.'

His laugh was short and sharp. 'Yes.'

'So? You think that means your wife—your real wife—would be automatically entitled to a huge share of that wealth?'

His eyes narrowed imperceptibly. 'It's a moot point, Alice. This will be my only wedding, you my only wife.'

'Why?' She stood, and then regretted it, when the simple action brought her body so close to his.

'Because I,' he said slowly, his eyes boring down on hers, the air between them suddenly crackling with an awareness that Alice assured herself was completely one-sided, 'am not made for marriage.' His smile covered a deeper confession, Alice was sure of it.

'In what way?' It was curiosity that fired her to ask it.

'In every way.' His own response was teasing, and she had a feeling he was hiding himself away from her, covering a truthful response with a glib joke.

Then again, who was she to pry? This wasn't a real marriage. They weren't even friends. It was business—purely business.

'So, all that is left now is to seal the deal.'

Alarm jolted down her spine, as for a moment, out of nowhere, the image of Thanos kissing her crashed into Alice's mind. Her knees began to tremble and her pulse was thready and inconsistent. Her eyes, when they lifted to his, were half shuttered, her lips parted in a breathy, silent, invitation she had no idea she was issuing.

'Seal the deal?' she heard herself whisper.

He made a throaty noise of agreement, and then took a step backwards, away from her, a desertion that had every single one of her senses screaming with disappointment.

'I thought we would go out.'

'Out?'

'Dancing. Getting your photo in the paper is the quickest way to let news of our engagement slip to the world.'

Alice's eyes shifted—reluctantly—from Thanos's face to the boulder she now wore on her finger, then to the reflective wall panel just a little way across the room. She'd come directly from the office and still wore an ill-fitting brown suit. It was hardly the stuff of elegant nightclubs, nor the kind of thing Thanos's real fiancée would, she presumed, be caught dead in.

'Dancing.' She found herself nodding. 'I can meet you at a club...'

He frowned. 'But you're right here.'

'I need to get changed first,' she pointed out, looking down at her figure.

His eyes narrowed and a smile played about

his lips. 'So you do.' Then, with a confident gesture of his tanned fingers, he motioned for her to join him as he strode through the penthouse.

Curious, she did exactly that, until he paused in the middle of a large, cream-coloured bedroom.

A dress was hanging against another door, a slinky red colour with spaghetti straps, made of silk, that she suspected would fall to mid-thigh, at best, and which looked to dip dangerously low over the cleavage.

It was the complete opposite of anything she'd ever buy for herself, and yet she found herself fascinated by its delicate construction, its beautiful design.

'This is for me?' She flicked her gaze to his in time to catch a hint of speculation in his eyes.

He nodded though, brusque and efficient. 'There are others,' he offered, 'but this is the one I liked best.' His wink did funny things to her gut. 'I'll be waiting outside.'

She nodded, not quite equal to making a verbal response, pulling the dress from the hanger a little uneasily and running her fingertips over the sensual material. A quick inspection of the wardrobe showed several other dresses, all of them designer, all somehow—mysteriously—in her size. Then again, Thanos was no doubt an expert in women's bodies—he could probably guess her measurements to within a millimetre's accuracy despite the fact he'd only ever seen her in business suits.

She scanned all of the dresses, and though there were some which were far more conservative and in keeping with her normal dress code, she found her attention continually returning to the strappy red he'd expressed a preference for. Finally, with a guttural noise of surrender, she undressed and pulled it on over her head, catching her reflection almost as soon as it had settled on her body.

And she froze.

Because Alice never wore anything revealing. She never showed more than a hint of cleavage, nor anything above the knee.

Her mother had been strict when Alice was growing up. *'Men are only ever after one thing, Alice Smart. Don't be like I was—fooled by any handsome man with a silver tongue.'*

And the one time Alice had defied her mother and gone out in a skimpy halter-neck top and miniskirt, she'd met Clinton—and everything her mother had said had been brought vividly to life.

Now, as a grown woman, and despite the fact Jane Smart was no longer able to deliver sermons on virtue and men's general failings, Alice remembered the lessons that had been drummed into her again and again, and chose to wear clothes that hid her figure completely.

This dress hid nothing.

And yet she liked it.

With a small smile on her pale pink lips, she dropped her gaze to the ring she wore and breathed out. Because she was 'engaged'. She wasn't going to fall prey to some guy who just wanted to get her into bed.

She was going out with the man she planned to marry. What did it matter that the marriage was a ruse?

Holding onto her determination, she fluffed her hair around her face, so it fell a little wild and abandoned, and pinched her cheeks until they had a pleasant flush.

Several pairs of high heels were lined up in the closet, and this time they were in different sizes, so when she settled on a pair that fitted—strappy sandals with a small heel—she felt a little like Cinderella.

Just as she began to contemplate what her own handbag would look like with this chic out-fit, she spied another wardrobe. A quick inspec-tion showed several handbags had been laid out on shelves, as well as jewellery that she knew—despite its glistening diamonds—wasn't cos-tume.

Swallowing, she grabbed a clutch purse that

matched the shoes, and turned to check her appearance one more time.

A stranger looked back at Alice.

A woman who was confident and in control. A woman who was *sexy*. The word came to Alice out of nowhere and a hive of bees seemed to take up residence in her belly, buzzing and swarming through her body.

Thanos was sexy.

He was sex appeal on a pair of very strong, long, lean legs.

She, Alice, was a fraud. A woman dressed up to play a part. And she needed to remember that; for her own sanity and emotional well-being, she couldn't let herself be suckered into this fantasy. She couldn't let herself believe, even for a moment, that this kind of thing could ever really happen to her.

It was just an act.

And soon, it would all be over.

She moved like an angel.

The discovery that his sensible, staid assistant actually had a killer figure and danced as though she'd been born with a beat inside her bones gave him the first tremor of alarm he'd felt since acquiescing to Leonidas's suggestion and proposing a marriage of convenience.

Alice had been easy to imagine as his wife.

Alice, as she'd been in the office, had been attractive in a way you'd never really notice. Nice face, nice eyes, nice smile, but there was nothing remarkable about her. He'd imagined her as the perfect bride to show Kosta how much he'd changed, without really demanding too much of Thanos's attention, once they were married.

But now, as she moved on the dance floor, her body being pushed close to his by the crush of people dancing around them, he began to see that perhaps he'd miscalculated.

She might not be anything like his usual lovers—blonde, leggy, slender and oftentimes dull as anything—but she was also nothing like he'd imagined either, and Thanos didn't generally like surprises. He dealt in known quantities and he had every reason to worry that Alice was not precisely that.

The music seemed to pulse through her, so she danced with her eyes shut, her generous lips pouted into a half-smile, half-hum, her arms moving rhythmically, and her breasts pushed against the fabric that had seemed like *such* a good idea at the time.

He moved his own body, hoping that it would distribute his blood a little more evenly throughout, rather than letting it pool in one limb only.

Her hips were mesmerising. She swayed and

rolled them as if it was second nature and the very unwelcome image of her completely naked, straddling him, rolling her hips in just this manner, filled his mind so he knew he was fighting a losing battle trying to bring his blood back to his body.

Theos. What was the matter with him? He went dancing with women all the time. He could control this. He had to.

Besides, he'd brought her here to be photographed, so word could get around that he was getting married. It was hardly going to work if he spent the whole night forcibly keeping her at arm's length so she wouldn't realise that desire was flooding his body.

'Thank you for this,' she said, lifting up onto tiptoes to offer the words closer to his ear. Her breasts brushed his torso and he had to pull back a little so she wouldn't feel the force of his arousal against her gut.

'For what?'

'For everything.' Her smile was quick to spread. He stared at it, desire like a drug now. 'Mom, mainly. But also for this. I haven't been dancing in a long time. I'd forgotten how much I love it.'

Her gratitude was the last thing he'd expected. He smiled, but knew it to be dismissive, and he felt her pull away from him, a hint of hurt on her features as she put a little physical space between them and began to dance once more.

He fought an urge to apologise and explain. This was business. Even this—the dancing—was a carefully staged photo op. And his body needed to remember that.

This wasn't a normal date. He wasn't going to take Alice home to his bed, seduce her all night until she screamed his name into his apartment, nor was he going to coax pleasure and euphoria from her, syllable by syllable.

Up until three days ago, she'd been his damned assistant. Up until three days ago, he hadn't known she existed. Not outside a voice at the end of the phone, or a name at the bottom of an email.

And she was definitely not his type.

Okay, tonight she looked a lot more like his type—only better. Fascinating. Rare. Unusual.

But Alice Smart was complicated. She moved in a completely different circle from him. He didn't need to look beyond the meagre requirements she'd voiced when they'd first negotiated their marriage bargain to know that they lived in different worlds.

Besides which, Thanos wasn't interested in a real relationship.

The very idea turned his blood to ice in his

veins. All his life, he'd known one thing with blinding clarity: *love stinks.*

If his own mother's decline hadn't proven that, then having a front-row seat to Dion and Maria's marriage breakup—a situation his arrival had caused—had definitely sent him the message with complete certainty.

People were born alone; they died alone. It was futile to try to live your life in a way that defied this. A marriage that would get him back a company he should never have lost seemed about the best thing Thanos could hope for.

So desiring Alice was utterly out of the question.

With the kind of discipline he'd brought to his business when it had gone completely pear-shaped, he forced his body to behave, concentrating on calming an over-excited member of his anatomy in particular, grinding his teeth until things were a little less heated, and then he smiled down at the woman he was going to marry.

The woman he'd arranged to marry purely because it made business sense. The woman he'd selected because she needed money, and money was the strongest motivator.

And he relaxed.

Because they both knew it was a commercial agreement. They both knew it was a contractual arrangement, nothing more. They both knew the terms, and were prepared to stick to them. Desire was neither here nor there in this marriage.

She was covered in a fine sheen of perspiration when they emerged from the nightclub two hours later, and she knew it made the dress cling to her even more. Knew, and didn't care. Her body was throbbing with pleasure and happiness, with a kind of light-heartedness she hadn't felt in a long time—if ever. When she was a child, they'd always been so stretched financially that their home had been tense, and Alice had borne that tension, had carried it inside her.

Then Jane had had her stroke and Alice's life had been plunged into an existence of worrying and stressing, of heartache and pain that she could rarely engage.

She couldn't remember the last time she'd simply danced. She couldn't remember the last time she'd smiled because happiness had been turning over inside her.

Everything was simple, and good, and she could relax a little.

A flash burst in her face, the light bright and blinding, and instinctively she curved her body closer to Thanos's, her expression shifting from a relaxed smile to a look of pure panic. She heard his curse, and remembered the main reason they'd come out tonight was to be photographed. They were here purely for this.

Why had she forgotten?

Fool! She should have at least checked her appearance in the cloakroom before leaving the bar.

'Got a live one, Thanos?' one of the paparazzi shouted, his accent cockney despite the fact they were in New York.

Thanos glared over Alice's head and then looked down into her face. She felt a strange, budding sense of calm despite this odd invasion of their privacy.

'You are sure about this?' he asked, quietly, his eyes roaming her face, giving her one last opportunity to pull out.

As if she could—even if this one very brief brush with his lifestyle had made her balk at what lay ahead. Thanks to his generosity, her mother was in a five-star care facility.

Thanks to Thanos, Alice would be living debt-free for the first time in years.

'I'm sure,' she agreed firmly.

'Okay, then.' He dipped his head forward and Alice had barely a second to get a grip of her emotions before his lips brushed hers. Just a quick buzz, skin on skin, an exhalation, and her pulse began to run riot in her veins, her skin prickling all over with goosebumps and anticipation.

Oh, my.

She lifted a hand to his chest, clinging to his shirt as though without his support she might topple to the ground, and unknowingly flashing her huge engagement ring for all the world to see. And see it they did, the photographers perched outside the Manhattan hotspot snapping furiously as they stayed clinging to one another, his body hard like a rock, hers soft and pliant. His hand curved around her back, resting just above the indentation of her spine, and his own breathing seemed ragged and out of control.

He was an excellent actor, because even as the moment threatened to drag every inch of sanity from her, there was still a small part of her that knew how run-of-the-mill this was for Thanos. How un-scintillating. How ordinary. This was a man who socialised with some of the most beautiful women in the world, who threw parties that Hollywood A-listers fought to attend.

He was hardly going to be truly moved by something as simple as a brushing of lips—and definitely not with someone like her.

If it weren't for the fact he was paying her handsomely, she'd have pulled away and put some distance between them. But this was an act, a charade, and she'd agreed to play her part.

So she moved her hand a little higher, curving

it over his shoulder to make sure the photographers behind them got a chance to glimpse the diamond. Only the act brought her body even closer, and as her flesh moulded to his she felt for herself all the proof she needed that he wasn't entirely unmoved by this.

His arousal was like a rock against her belly and her harsh intake of breath was evidence that she'd felt it. Her eyes slid to his and her heart began to churn, because a drum was beating, slow and steady but unstoppably, and it was pulling Alice towards it, demanding she listen, and then that she answer.

'Let's go home.' The throaty command came to her as if on delay. She heard his words, struggled to compute them, and finally nodded.

Home.

With her fiancé.

Her body trembled as he put a hand in the small of her back and guided her to a waiting limousine, opening the rear door for her and using his own body to cover hers as she stepped into the car in a dress that was too small to accomplish such a manoeuvre easily.

A second later, he was in the space with her, and the air seemed to crackle as though lightning were whipping between them.

Ten minutes ago, this had seemed simple. And then he'd kissed her, and her brain had fired

up and her body had begun to feel things it had
no business feeling and Alice could have sworn
she was tipping right off the edge of the earth.

CHAPTER FIVE

HE SHOULDN'T HAVE kissed her.

Thanos lay in his bed, on his back, staring at the ceiling, unable to sleep, unable to get Alice Smart from his mind.

The kiss had been a mistake.

Sure, he'd wanted to get papped. He'd wanted a photo of them in all the papers and on all the blogs in the morning. He'd wanted to hit Kosta with a one-two-surprised-you when next they spoke.

But kissing Alice?

Hell.

He'd opened a can of worms.

Dancing with her had been bad enough, but feeling her body pressed to his, capturing her lips, feeling her rush of warm breath, tasting her sweetness. Every single nuance of that interaction replayed in his mind now.

The feel of her body, warm and moist from dancing, her hair—the way it had smelled, like wildflowers on a sunny field. The way her fingers had knotted in his shirt, clinging to him as if she were drowning, the way her eyes had flown to his, filled with a surge of desire powerful enough to rob them both of breath.

It had taken every ounce of his legendary self-control to have his driver take Alice to her own home, to walk her to the door without going anywhere near enough to touch her—even by mistake.

Come home with me.

The words had rushed through his brain, demanding to be spoken, but thank *Christós* his tongue had obeyed him, refusing to offer an invitation that would only serve to complicate matters.

He groaned as his body tightened, growing hard beneath the sheet, so he thrust the thought away, pushing out of bed and striding to the windows that overlooked Manhattan.

This had the potential to be a total disaster if he didn't control it.

He had no intention of really marrying a woman—ever—and that was why this marriage would work so well! It was business. Business, business, business.

Except it wasn't.

Or rather, it wouldn't be, if he didn't take very great care to keep a lid on his desire for her, and to ensure she did the same.

With a roll of his eyes and a guttural moan, he

wondered if it was too late to insert a non-consummation clause in their marriage contracts. A threat that she'd void everything if they slept together.

It wasn't exactly unreasonable, but the second the thought occurred to him, he dismissed it. And that alone should have given him a mountain of doubt.

Because he wasn't fighting hard enough to control this—and Thanos always fought for what he wanted.

Sydney Harbour glistened before him. He kicked back on his yacht, staring out at the world-famous skyline, glad he'd had business here in Australia to take him away from Alice. After the night at the club, he'd needed some space. The kind of space he couldn't get in a city like Manhattan. True, it was teeming with more than one and a half million people, but there was one who kept drawing his focus, distracting him when he could really do without it.

And so, Sydney.

He'd always loved this city for its mix of old and new, for its air of entrepreneurialism and elitism, its egalitarian spirit. And he loved it now for being a port in the storm.

A reprieve.

A bolthole.

Yes, he'd run away.

He'd had an envelope delivered to Alice at home the morning after the club, containing his credit card and a list of things he suggested she buy. Clothes, shoes, bags, jewels, all the things his wife would be required to have on hand, as well as some things she might not think of, which only she could deal with, such as updating her passport.

And then, he'd left the country without daring to see her again.

It was too risky.

He didn't want to complicate this.

Their arrangement had been perfect, and it still would be. They both just needed to get used to what they'd agreed to, to remember the reasons it made sense to keep things on a certain level, and everything would be fine.

Alice stroked her mother's hand, wondering when her skin had become so papery, and tears cloyed her throat.

'I bought my wedding dress today, Mom.' She lifted her gaze to her mother's face, as always, looking for a hint of recognition, anything that might suggest Jane had heard a word of what was being said. 'It's beautiful. You'd love it. Or maybe you'd hate it,' Alice said in a voice that was half apology, half amusement.

The dress had cost a fortune, but once she'd started looking on the Internet for inspiration, scouring the weddings of people 'like' Thanos—not that there were many—she'd realised she'd have to up her game and buy something a little more luxurious than the chain-store gown she'd been eyeing.

Besides, these wedding photos would be printed in huge publications. She needed to look as if she'd gone to an appropriate degree of effort.

'It's so nice.' Nice? What a bland word for the stunning creation. A spectacular bodice fitted to her torso, sculpting her breasts in a way that even Alice had to admit was flattering, flaring into a big tulle skirt that was like something out of a fairy tale. The front was all Cinderella but the back was next-level sexy.

So much so, she'd almost resisted trying it on, but the stylist had been insistent and the second Alice had been buttoned into it, she'd gasped, because the stylist was right: it was perfect. Completely backless, it showed Alice's elegant figure to advantage, her creamy skin just the right shade to complement the crisp white of the dress.

'I wish you could be at the wedding,' she said honestly, thinking of how strange it would be to get married without her mother there. How utterly surreal to stand up in front of hundreds of people and say her vows to a man she'd only met a week or so ago, a man who most women would give their eye-teeth to marry.

Jane Smart lay completely still, as she had done ever since her stroke, and Alice sat beside her, gently padding a thumb over her mother's hand, knowing, without any reason to believe it, that being there meant something to Jane. That her mother *knew* Alice was with her and was glad.

'It's not too late to pull out of this,' Leonidas, murmured out of the side of his mouth.

Thanos looked around the packed marquee at the four hundred guests who'd travelled deep into the Provençal countryside on incredibly short notice to attend the nuptials of Europe's most famous and established bachelor.

'You don't think?'

Leonidas grinned, shrugging his shoulders. 'You're Thanos Stathakis. You can do whatever the hell you want.'

Thanos discounted the idea immediately. This made sense. Almost two weeks apart from Alice had reminded him of the professionalism required by this arrangement. She'd worked for him in one capacity for six months; this wasn't really hugely different. It was a business arrangement, pure and simple.

'What I want is to buy Petó,' he reminded Leonidas softly, turning his gaze on his brother's face. 'And Alice is the key to that.'

'Speaking of which, Kosta Carinedes is here. Did you see?'

Thanos lifted a brow, a smile quirking his lips. 'This whole thing is for his benefit. Did you think I would not invite him?'

Leonidas shook his head ruefully. 'You really are too good at this.'

Thanos shrugged, his expression like steel as the purpose for this marriage firmed in his mind. 'I've spent way too much time on P & A to lose it now.'

'After this, I imagine it is in the bag.'

'Let's hope so.'

'What's she like, anyway?'

Alice.

He frowned, trying to think of the words to describe his one-time assistant. Efficient. Pragmatic. No nonsense. And yet, she wasn't really, was she?

All it had taken was a few hours' dancing, the quickest kiss, and they'd both gone up in flames.

His pulse lifted now, his body temperature climbing in anticipation of seeing his bride, and he had to work double time to tamp down on the response. 'She's…unusual.'

'Unusual? Does she have three heads?'

Thanos bared his teeth in an imitation of a smile. 'I mean, she's not my usual type.'

'Naturally. This isn't your usual wedding though, is it?'

'No,' Thanos was quick to agree.

'You like her, though?'

Thanos shook his head, desperate to refute that suggestion. 'It's just business.'

'Are you sure?' Leonidas's eyes rested on his brother's profile thoughtfully.

'Absolutely certain. As soon as I have the contract for P & A, this marriage is over and I'll likely never see my "wife" again.'

'And she's okay with that?'

'Okay with it? She's thrilled. We both are. That's the deal we've struck.'

Remembering the deal was important. He invoked it now as a talisman to the purpose for this wedding, smiling with an air of relaxation that he didn't completely feel.

The eleven members of the French Philharmonic Orchestra, who'd been instructed to play pre-ceremony music, brought their piece softly to a close, and silence began to descend upon the marquee.

It reigned for only a moment before the famous strains of the wedding march began to play, the music robust and beautiful.

Thanos's eyes moved with a sort of desperate

fatalism towards the entrance, his whole body on alert for this moment. He reminded himself he was supposed to look like a man in love, a man waiting to see a woman he adored, and he pasted a look on his face that he hoped passed for doting—and tried not to think how much genuine anticipation there was in his body at that moment.

The instant Alice appeared, he found it almost impossible to conceal his true reaction. Several things hit him all at once.

She was walking down the aisle alone. This he had expected. He knew from their conversations that her mother was obviously bedridden, and, from the light background check Leonidas had insisted Thanos run, that her father was a mystery. No one was named on her birth certificate, no one had shared legal custody of Alice, certainly there was no one in her life who'd acted the part of father.

And there were no siblings.

He hadn't expected, therefore, that she would be accompanied down the aisle, and yet the sight of her on her own did something strange to his gut, pulling at it mercilessly, so he fought an impulse to push a hand against the wall of his stomach.

She was alone.

Just like him.

They were born alone, they died alone, and they were marrying—alone.

It wasn't just the sight of her stepping slowly towards him, with no other human to keep her company, that made his breath labour in his lungs.

As she walked purposefully up the aisle, he couldn't help but realise how little she resembled the no-nonsense assistant he'd propositioned.

Just like the night at the club, Alice Smart had transformed into something and someone completely different. This time, she was less sex siren and more Princess-in-Waiting. The dress was utterly spectacular, though he suspected on its hanger, or on another woman, it would barely catch his eye. But worn by Alice, it was a piece of mastery, flattering her body, teasing with every shift of fabric, making him want to touch it, to touch her, to feel every single inch of the fabric, and what was beneath.

Then there was the veil. While the dress was beautifully crafted and made him ache to examine it in greater detail, the veil was like something other-worldly. Made of tulle, it had a fine lace edging and on closer inspection he saw that flowers had been etched into the fabric, and, at each edge, a very fine cluster of diamonds was stitched into it. He stared at her through the gauze, the lurching in his gut entirely unwelcome and inappropriate.

'Hi.'

Her softly voiced word had sanity surge back inside him, because he heard her trepidation and nervousness and realised what a jerk he was being to be focussing on the fact she looked impossibly, tantalisingly beautiful. This was a *huge* deal for Alice. Sure, it was a fake wedding, but that didn't change the fact that the world's elite had flown in to watch them say their vows; it didn't change the fact there were television helicopters buzzing overhead, that the media had camped at the end of the private road that led to this hotel estate.

It didn't change the fact that this was her wedding day and she was way out of her comfort zone. As was he, come to think of it, but he stood to gain immensely from this wedding.

He smiled—reassuringly, he hoped—and put a hand out for her. She placed her own in it, her fingertips trembling, so he squeezed and tucked her hand in his.

'You ready?' he asked quietly, leaning towards her. And as with outside the nightclub, she blinked her eyes up to him and nodded. Fearless, even when he suspected she truly was afraid.

The ceremony was short enough—just the

vows, the legal stuff, and finally, the invitation that he may now kiss his bride.

His bride.

He looked towards Alice and studied her face in profile, wondering at the wisdom of this, simultaneously knowing it was too late to change a thing.

Remembering their audience, and one man in particular, he put an arm around her waist and drew her close enough to whisper so only Alice could hear, 'It's show time, Mrs Stathakis.'

The words were teasing, intended to be light-hearted, but there was nothing light-hearted about being close to Alice. Nothing light-hearted about the way passion soared through him, desire hammering against his body like a call he must answer.

He had just a moment to see her eyes widen and surprise flare in their depths before he kissed her.

It was a performance, an act. Except, it wasn't.

True, Kosta Carinedes was there watching, as well as four hundred other interested people, but Thanos pulled Alice into his arms and kissed her as though he was picking up right where they'd left off outside the nightclub.

He kissed her as if there were no one else in the marquee, he kissed her with all the desire that had been firing between them since he'd walked into his office in New York and come face to face with the woman who'd reorganised his life and dealt with every possible query he could throw at her.

He kissed her and his arms came around her bare back, so he groaned when he felt her naked flesh beneath his fingertips, holding her tight to his body, his kiss deepening even when he knew he ought to pull back, to lift his head, to give them both space to breathe. Right when he was about to do so, she pushed her own body closer, as though she too couldn't get enough of this, her hips shifting a little from one side to the other, just as they had in the club, moving so perfectly, so sweetly, that he ached for her in a way he recognised as pure white-hot desire, and from which he knew he needed to run a thousand miles.

Except this felt so good. So right.

He couldn't help but surrender to it, for just a little longer.

Besides, if Kosta Carinedes had any doubts whatsoever about the veracity of this hastily arranged marriage, then he imagined they were quickly fading into nothing.

Telling himself it was purely for the older man's benefit, he gave up trying to fight the kiss and he gave into it entirely. His tongue duelled with hers, his chest moved in time with Alice's, their breathing in unison as they exploded—

simultaneously—in a moment of passion that could only have been better if there had been a bed within easy reach.

'You used to work for him, didn't you?'

Alice blinked up, her eyes chasing the question. The wedding reception was taking place in the grand ballroom of the Stathakis hotel, and there were at least twice the guests in attendance as had been at the ceremony itself. Trays of locally produced champagne were circulating in cut-crystal glasses and the hors d'oeuvres had all been exceptional. An enormous oyster bar stood in the corner, brimming with the crustacean, which could be enjoyed *au natural* or with any number of additions—beluga caviar, sour cream and smoked salmon, bacon and Worcestershire sauce.

Alice turned away from the incredible display to regard the woman who'd approached her, who was asking how she knew Thanos. She was tall, skinnier than a beanpole, dressed in silky couture with perfect make-up, perfect nails, and long blonde hair that had been curled into loose waves, which now hung with artful elegance around her face.

'Yes,' Alice responded, hiding her uneasiness with a look that could freeze ice. She didn't bother smiling—she didn't need to move in these social circles to see the way these women were looking at her.

As if she didn't belong. As if she'd come in and taken some kind of prize from their laps.

Of their own accord, her eyes skipped across the room, not stopping until they found him in the crowd. Despite her repeated mental reminders that this was just a job, a performance, her stomach did a funny little lurch at the sight he made.

There, in the middle of the polished marble floor, he was dancing, but not with any one of the glamorous women making eyes at him. Thanos had a little girl in his arms, and he was twirling her around the room, his eyes crinkled in the corners with laughter, as she held on tight and giggled.

She'd been introduced to Leonidas's wife Hannah and their eighteen-month-old Isabella earlier in the day. She'd never really thought of Thanos as someone with family—even though she knew the bare details. His father was in prison, and of course his brother was his business partner; they owned their enterprise together.

But seeing Thanos with these people humanised him in a dangerous way, in a way she didn't welcome. It made her want to know more about him. To ask him questions about his life growing up, about his relationship with his brother and sister-in-law, to know more than the bare facts of his father's imprisonment, and more than she could find on the Internet. She wanted to know how Thanos had *felt*. How he had survived such an awful phase of his life.

It was easier for Alice to think of him as a billionaire tycoon—successful, arrogant, fiercely intelligent and determined. It was easier for her to think of him as the 'playboy prince of Europe', to remember he had a reputation for taking women to bed with the same kind of regularity with which most people changed underwear.

Seeing him play with a little girl, though, added another dimension to his personality. One Alice wasn't entirely sure she wanted to recognise.

'It's strange,' the blonde beside her continued. 'I was with him only a few weeks ago and he never mentioned you.'

'I'm not surprised,' Alice murmured, figuring there wasn't much more she could say.

'You must be pregnant,' the woman continued thoughtfully. 'That would make sense.' She dragged her gaze over Alice's body questioningly.

'If I am, it would be news to me.'

'I just think it's weird that he never spoke about you.'

Alice's gut lurched at the lie they were perpetuating. This woman's confusion was easy to understand. This wedding had come out of the blue—for all of them.

'We wanted to keep it private,' she murmured. 'The media can be such a pain.'

'Don't I know it,' the blonde agreed, and Alice found herself softening towards the other woman a little. 'You get used to it eventually. Sort of.'

Alice nodded, even though she knew there'd be no need to get used to it. Not in the long term. Sooner rather than later, this marriage would be ended, and Alice would go back to her real life, her real self. As much as possible, anyway, given that she'd be a millionaire.

At that moment, Thanos tilted his head and his eyes caught Alice, and everything inside her went completely off-balance. Anticipation was a tsunami inside her and it was dragging her forward and sucking her under. She was losing all of herself in that moment, losing everything she knew about herself, everything she'd ever thought. She stared at him, powerless to look away, even when the blonde began speaking again.

'You'll have to come away with us next time we sail.'

'Oh?' Alice was going through the motions of the conversation now. Her body was pulling her forward, onto the dance floor, begging her to move to her groom's side.

He hadn't looked away and Alice was drowning in the depths of his eyes.

'A big group of us go a few times a year. It's fine. Lots of champagne. Sunshine. Too much food.' The woman—about the size of a pencil—grimaced, but Alice didn't see the gesture.

'Sounds fun,' she said, wondering in the back of her mind if she'd even be around when the next trip took place.

'He's a real catch, you know,' the woman said on a small sigh. Alice nodded, and in that moment she rather suspected he might be.

For someone else.

The words rushed through her body, jolting her back to reality.

Not for Alice.

Never for Alice.

He had laid all his cards out on the table. This was just business. Nothing personal. He didn't want this to be anything more than a business transaction.

Whatever desire was zapping between them simply had to be controlled.

And it was more than just Thanos's wishes. Alice had learned her lesson at her mother's side and then again when she'd briefly let her own guard down, she'd paid the price with a heart that had been shattered well beyond repair. At least, well beyond a point that would allow her to trust again.

He lifted a hand, beckoning her slowly towards him, and she straightened, schooling her breath into a soft, gentle pattern, telling herself this was just a performance and that she must, as he'd said during the ceremony, play her part.

'Excuse me,' she murmured, turning a vague smile in the direction of the wedding guest she'd been speaking to. 'I'm going to dance with my husband.'

CHAPTER SIX

IT WAS EVERY bit as troubling as dancing with her in the nightclub had been. More so, because now Alice was his wife. Mrs Stathakis. And despite all the promises he'd made himself over the years, his utter certainty he would never do anything so foolish as marry, he felt an odd puffing of his chest when he thought of Alice in those terms.

She moved in his arms so perfectly, her body moulded to his, and his hands roamed her back distractedly, feeling the smoothness of her skin, the ridges of her spine.

'Do you actually know all these people?' she murmured, looking up at him so he tilted his head down to hers. Their eyes locked and for a moment his dancing slowed.

He started moving again, swirling her around gently. 'Most of them. Why?'

Her smile was self-deprecating. 'It's just so many people. It's kind of overwhelming.'

'I don't know many of them well,' he amended honestly.

'So they're mostly business associates?'

Thanos considered that. 'Many are, yes. But I suppose a few hundred are people I socialise with.'

'But aren't actually friends with?' she prompted, a teasing smile on her face, a divot between her brows that he had an irrational urge to drop his lips to and kiss.

'What's your definition of a friend?'

'Someone you could call at any time, day or night, who'd have your back when you needed support.'

He lifted a brow, his stomach churning a little. 'In that case, I have only one friend.'

'Oh?'

He swivelled his head, moving his gaze across the room. 'My brother, Leonidas.'

'Ah.' Her smile was just a lift at the corners. 'I think that's cheating.'

He laughed, a sound that ruffled through his broad chest. 'Is it?'

'Yep. And I can't compete because I have no siblings, so it's not really fair.'

'You didn't invite any of your friends?'

She pulled her mouth to the side a bit, as she thought about that. 'I don't really have any friends.'

He saw regret cross her face followed swiftly by confusion, almost as though she'd said more than she'd intended, and wanted to draw the words back in. But he wouldn't let her. Her admission fascinated him.

'Why not?'

'Honestly?'

'Yeah.'

'It's complicated.'

He arched a brow. 'I'm your husband, remember.'

She pulled a face and lowered her voice, lifting up onto the tips of her toes so he alone would hear her. 'In name only.'

'Ah.' He grinned. 'Don't hold that against me.'

Alice lowered her body back, staying close to him, her brow furrowed thoughtfully. 'I'll try not to.'

'So? Friends?'

She expelled a soft sigh. 'We moved around a lot when I was growing up. It was hard to meet friends, and once I did, we'd leave town again. I used to email a few, but after about my sixth school, I stopped even trying to learn the names.' She grimaced. 'Work is no different. I mean, I'm a temp, so by the very nature of my job, I'm never in the same place for long. And when I am, and I do by chance come across someone I click with socially, I can't really catch up with them because I care for Mom so much of the time.'

Thanos hadn't been born with the proverbial

silver spoon in his mouth. True, he'd known excessive wealth and comfort during his childhood, but he'd also known a corresponding degree of pain and emotional distance, of loss and hardship, and yet he found it hard to think of a single thing he'd gone through that could compare to the sheer loneliness of what Alice had experienced.

'I'm only twenty-four but I don't really do the stuff people my age are into. I can't afford it.'

He smiled but it was completely without humour.

'There wasn't anyone I could think of to invite,' she said with a lift of her shoulders.

'I'm sorry.'

'Please don't be,' she said with a shake of her head and a slightly tremulous smile. 'If you're going to feel sorry for me, feel sorry for me because my dad never wanted to know me or because my mom is in a coma, or because I had a credit-card debt the size of Mount Everest until you entered the picture. I can live without friends.'

He slowed his dancing once more, thinking again how similar they were, how independent, how determined to show that they were okay with being on their own.

'I'm sorry for those things, too.' He stared down at her, wondering at the twists and turns life had served this woman, at the reality she'd been forced to live, and sympathy tore through him.

But she smiled, and even if it didn't reach her eyes, it totally changed her face.

'It's our wedding day,' she reminded him. 'We should look happy, not glum.'

Before he could reply, they were interrupted by the arrival of Kosta Carinedes.

'Thanos,' he said with a nod, his eyes shifting to Alice's with obvious interest. 'Miss Smart.'

'Mrs Stathakis,' Alice corrected without missing a beat, tilting her face towards Thanos's and smiling in a way that was now a perfect imitation of a woman madly in love. And even though she was simply pretending, something like warmth spread through Thanos, starting at his chest and radiating out through his body in waves.

'Of course.' Kosta still seemed as if he was waiting for the punchline. He looked from one to the other with a sense of bemusement.

'We're so glad you could join us,' Alice enthused, going over the top of his doubts with a truly gifted performance. 'I felt quite bad the other day, when you came to the office and we didn't confess the truth.'

Thanos's eyes narrowed.

'So this was going on then?'

Alice arched a brow teasingly. 'We just got

married,' she pointed out. 'Of course it was going on then.'

'So you've been an item for some time?'

Thanos stroked Alice's side without realising he was doing it. 'We wanted to keep things quiet for as long as possible. You know, privacy concerns.'

'Naturally.' Kosta's eyes narrowed. 'How long have you been dating?' he prompted, like a dog with a bone, refusing to give up on his inquisition.

Thanos ground his teeth together, pushing his impatience aside. 'It feels like a very long time ago that I first saw Alice and lost my heart.'

Alice's expression showed surprise as she looked at him, so he stroked her side, and slowly she smiled, turning back to Kosta. 'I understand your concerns about my husband, Mr Carinedes. But it's important to remember that newspapers will write a story about just about anything.'

Kosta considered this for a moment. 'That is true, m'dear. Very true.'

They were quiet for a moment, and Thanos had to bite back an impulse to ask the older man when he intended to sign the company over to him— surely his last objection had been dealt with?

'You're having a honeymoon?' Kosta asked, and Thanos could tell he'd surprised Alice when he nodded in the affirmative.

'That is the norm, is it not?' Thanos prompted.

'Of course. Where will you go?'

Thanos turned to Alice, a smile on his face. 'It's a surprise, for my bride.'

'Ah.' This appeared to please the old man. He clapped his hands together and offered the first genuine smile Thanos had seen from him in a long time. 'Well, when it's over, why don't you two join me in Port D'Angelo for an evening?'

'Port D'Angelo?' Alice prompted.

'A small town on the southern coast of Kalatheros—my home is there. Come—see the ocean, eat *galaktoboureko* and drink wine. I would enjoy getting to know you better, Alice.'

Thanos smiled, but he read the subtext. This would be a test. A 'throwing down of the gauntlet' to make sure their marriage was the real deal. He couldn't blame the older man for taking the precaution. The circumstances were highly suspicious—and with good reason.

'Fine.' Alice's smile was completely relaxed. She was clearly an excellent actress—better even than he'd suspected. 'I'd like that. Thanos?'

'We'll come as soon as we can,' Thanos murmured.

'Shall we say a week?'

'A week?' Thanos balked at that, for no reason he could think of. 'Make it three.'

Beside him Alice stiffened, and lifted her face

to his. 'Don't be silly, Thanos. A week is fine.' Her smile was encouraging, and he couldn't have said why but he felt annoyed. Impatient.

'Good,' Kosta rolled on, their acquiescence now apparently something he took for granted. But he sobered, his expression growing serious as he looked up at Thanos. 'She is your family now. All that you do is for her.'

The wedding dress *on* Alice had been bad enough. But it was somehow so much worse when he stepped into the luxurious bathroom of the hotel penthouse to see it carefully arranged over a coat hanger, suspended from the gold frame of the shower screen.

He ran his fingers over the lace bodice, as he'd been aching to do all day, his gut tightening with memories of how Alice had looked *in* the dress. And imagining how she looked *out* of it.

He stifled a groan, washing his face and unbuttoning his own shirt, discarding it considerably less carefully, in a pile on the floor. He braced his palms on the marble counter and stared at his reflection, a haunted look in his eyes as he noted the detail of the gold band on his wedding finger.

He was married.

And it didn't matter that it was just a sham, he felt a panicking constriction in his chest, rising to his throat, making breathing momentarily difficult.

Married.

Just as he'd sworn he'd never be.

He swept his eyes shut for a moment, inhaling, exhaling, ignoring the panic, focussing on the end result of this.

Petó. The company that would be his.

It didn't matter that he'd got way more than he'd bargained for with Alice Smart. It didn't matter that he'd suggested this when he'd thought her efficiency outstripped any other quality she possessed, when he'd thought she'd be a convenient bride—convenient in that he'd barely notice she was around.

How wrong he'd been!

He was noticing her, noticing her in all the ways he didn't want to.

The brief kiss at the nightclub had been bad, but he'd been able to tame it. The kiss at their wedding? It had pulled at every single one of his senses and even now his body was on fire, wanting to know how that kiss would end if they gave it free rein.

A noise from beyond the bathroom had him moving to the door, and when he stepped out, it was to see Alice in the kitchen, filling a kettle with water.

And desire throbbed low in his abdomen, refusing to be quelled. Because the wedding dress had been impressive, but even now, with her face wiped of make-up, her dark hair loose around her face, dressed in a simple T-shirt and pants that looked to be stretchy yoga tights, she was working her way into his mind, so he couldn't look away, and couldn't think of anything else.

He must have made a noise without realising it, because she lifted her face, her eyes locking to his in surprise, her lips parting a little.

'I didn't know you were in here.'

The kiss had been fascinating.

He hadn't expected such a depth of response from her, nor had he expected to want her in a way that had robbed him of any common sense.

Thanos stood on a precipice now. Common sense and safety were on one side, and on the other, something far more dangerous and infinitely more pleasing.

'I...' A furrow developed between her brows. 'I thought I'd go to bed. With a cup of tea. And a book.' Her breath moved quickly, her chest lifting with each huff, so her nipples strained against the flimsy cotton material of her shirt and he wondered what she'd feel like. If he reached his hands out and curved them over her breasts...

He banished the thought from his mind and waited for her to make her tea and leave.

Except she didn't. She poured the water into

a cup and stayed right where she was, her eyes roaming his face slowly, hungrily, as though she too was reluctant to put distance and sleep between them. As if this day—their wedding day—was somehow magical and apart from regular time.

'So...' She let the word hang between them, a little puff of air, a question, an answer, an invitation.

'So.' His smile was slow to spread across his face.

'A honeymoon?' she prompted, lifting her tea to her lips and sipping it, cupping it with both hands. Her wedding ring shone like a beacon of light.

'Isn't that traditional?'

'For real couples,' she said with a note to her voice that could have been wistful, and could have been teasing.

'This has to look like a real marriage,' he reminded her. 'The world will expect us to be revelling in our "happy couple" life.'

She pulled a face, and pushed up from the bench at the same time, coming around to stand beside him. 'You don't really seem like someone who'd care what the world thinks.'

His laugh was just a harsh sound of agreement. 'Generally I don't.' He didn't add that more often than not he lived to defy expectations, not to meet them.

'So this is all for Kosta's sake?'

He tilted his head towards hers, unable to explain why he wanted to deny that. He fought the temptation, and nodded instead. 'Yes, *agape*.'

'This company—'

'Petó.'

She nodded. 'It obviously means a lot to you.'

'Yes.'

'But you have lots of other companies.'

'This was my grandfather's.'

She tilted her head to the side, a gesture he now knew to mean she was considering something. Only it put sensible thought right out of his mind, so all he could do was look at the delicate curve of her neck, the creaminess of her skin. Desire kicked up a notch and he felt as though the air between them were crackling with heat and fire.

He had to fight it.

Didn't he?

'He had a lot of businesses?'

'Yes. But not like Petó.'

'Why not?'

'It was his favourite.' He made light of the question, lifting a hand and rubbing it across the back of his neck. 'It was his father's before him. When I first came to live with Dion, it was our grandfather who spent time with us. With me.'

His voice deepened on the admission. 'I think perhaps he saw what no one else did.'

'What's that?'

He forced a smile to his face to compensate for the maudlin response. 'I was alone. Completely alone. And terrified.'

'You?' she teased, but she was faking it too, he could tell. Sympathy softened her eyes, and she lifted a hand to his chest, so he drew in a deep breath as she pressed her palm over his heart. 'Surely you were never afraid of anything?'

'Only a fool lives without fear,' he commented softly.

She bit down on her lip. 'That's very true.'

He lifted his hand, laying it over hers, his eyes locked to hers, daring her to say something, to do something, to pull away and put a stop to this. She didn't.

His heart was pounding, slamming against his ribs, and the pull of his desire refused to be ignored. He pushed his body up, just enough to bring them into contact, and with his spare hand he removed her teacup, reaching behind him and placing it on the bench.

'You were going to bed,' he said quietly, not sure if he was suggesting she leave, or angling for an invitation to join her.

She nodded, her eyes locked to his. 'I know.' And she lifted up onto the tips of her toes once more, her body—so soft with gentle curves in all the most fascinating places—pressing against him so he wanted to lift her up and lay her down on the kitchen bench, to take her then and there. Except that felt completely wrong, even more so than just wanting to take her to bed.

Hadn't he sworn this wouldn't be a real marriage?

And it still wouldn't be. Even if they were to succumb to this, they both knew what was on offer—and, more importantly, what wasn't.

This was a business relationship, first and foremost. Nothing that happened between them would alter the parameters of that.

'How did your grandfather help you?'

The question surprised him. He ignored it, at first. He no longer wanted to think about his family. Nor to talk about them. All his focus was on this moment, and the woman pressed against him.

A voice from the back of his mind was shouting at him to put an end to this, but it was being swamped by other, more desirable inclinations. Inclinations that were so much easier and more pleasurable to obey.

Her hand ran across his naked chest and he closed his eyes for a moment, inhaling deeply, breathing in her fragrance, the sweetness of it, the innocence, and his gut rolled.

'Thanos?'

He didn't know if she was prompting him about her earlier question, or asking him what the hell was happening.

He jerked his eyes open and stared down at her, and a roll of something like dissatisfaction went through him, a roll of betrayal, because it hadn't been supposed to happen like this. Their wedding was meant to be rational and sensible—their marriage easy to control. They'd both said as much when they'd agreed to enter into this.

Now? He wanted to shift the goalposts, and he needed her to agree to that.

'I know we said this would be a business arrangement...' He curved his hands around her hips, lifting her shirt a little so he could feel her bare flesh. Her eyes swept shut, her lashes forming two perfect, dark crescents against the creamy pale of her cheeks.

'We did.' Her words were so throaty they were almost impossible to discern.

He lifted a hand to her cheek, holding it in his palm, staring down at her.

'This doesn't feel businesslike.'

He padded his thumb to her lip, anguish torturing him, the wait an agony. 'I have no interest in relationships.'

Her eyes flared a little wider, but she was still. Watchful. Listening.

'I don't ever lie about that. I do not believe in leading anyone on.'

She nodded, swallowing, darting her tongue out to lick the corner of her mouth. His arousal strained hard against his pants.

'Nothing that happens between us will change what I want from you. Our marriage is a construct to enable me to buy a company that I consider to be my birthright. That's all.'

She nodded slowly and made no effort to move away from him.

'But, *agape mou*, I am full of longing for you, and all I can think about is making you mine. Just for this night. Just once.'

A strangled noise escaped her throat, a sound of acquiescence, he thought, but he needed to be sure. He dropped his hands to his sides, holding his body completely still, his nostrils flaring with the strength of his breathing as he stared at her, waiting, impatient, desperately hungry. 'Tell me you understand,' he commanded. 'No.' He shook his head. 'Tell me you want what I want.'

Silence crackled between them, and he waited, each second like a torturous beat in time that was hammering against him.

'I want...' She paused, and he had no idea if she was intentionally torturing him, or if it was by accident, but, either way, he felt impatience burst through him like a physical force, strong enough to threaten the very fabric of his soul. 'This one night,' she continued shakily, and before he could respond she lifted a finger to his lips, keeping him silent. 'One night, no strings, no questions, no promises.'

And if those limitations sounded a little bit sad, the brightness of her smile contradicted that sentiment. She dropped her hand and looked up at Thanos as though he were everything she'd been waiting for.

And for that night, he really, really wanted to be.

CHAPTER SEVEN

His hands on her body were gentle, roaming her flesh slowly, so slowly, feeling every little bit of her. Her arms, where his touch sparked a torrent of nerve endings and goosebumps, her shoulders, his fingers splayed wide, his thumbs moving to the base of her neck, his eyes locked to hers, always watching, examining, seeing the way she responded.

Reading her, as though she were a book. And she stood there, looking up at him, her eyes huge in her face, her expression stricken—not with panic, so much as a sense of wild longing, and surprise that she could feel that. Surprise that he could invoke that.

She'd thought Clinton had inured her to sexual attraction.

She'd thought she'd learned how stupid it was to let your body guide you like this.

But standing there with Thanos Stathakis lifting her shirt higher up her body, she felt only relief.

'You're trembling.' His hands grazed her

sides, the fabric soft against her oversensitive skin.

'I know.' She nodded, and when he pushed her shirt over her breasts, his palms grazing the sensitive flesh of her nipples, she moaned softly, the feeling like nothing she'd ever known before.

He pushed it over her head and dropped it to the floor at their feet then returned his hands to her breasts, cupping them lightly while dropping his head, his lips seeking hers, kissing her with a slow inquiry.

It was like lighting a fuse.

Desire exploded inside Alice, a spark igniting to a firework, so she was pushing up onto the bench, sitting against it, her legs wrapped around his waist, her hands desperately running over his chest and back, seeking skin, needing to feel it beneath her fingertips, to feel *him* beneath her.

'I didn't expect this.' She kissed the admission into his mouth, wondering in the back of her mind if it was true. Hadn't she looked at Thanos from that first morning and felt a kick of longing? Still, their wedding was supposed to be a means to an end—and not this end.

In response he kissed her harder, his mouth crushing hers, his fingers weaving through her hair, cupping her scalp, holding her in place for his total domination, his body weight easing her back, so she was lying on the cold marble bench top, his hair-roughened torso a torture against her sensitive nipples. She arched her back, lifting her hips in a silent, age-old invitation, and he laid a line of kisses from her lips to her throat, flicking her décolletage with his tongue, so she moaned into the night air, the word 'please' tripping out of her mouth again and again.

Ancient, primal urges drove her and she answered their call, her body wild, her breathing ragged. She dug her heels into his back, drawing him closer to her feminine heart, and his hands dropped to the yoga pants she wore, pushing inside the elastic and cupping her bottom,. He lifted her, pulling her from the bench, so she wrapped her arms around his neck and kissed him as he carried her through the palatial lounge towards a large leather ottoman.

It was jet black outside the windows—vineyards rolled away from the hotel and in the distance there was the ocean, waves relentlessly pounding against the shoreline, just as need was slashing against her heart, demanding she answer it.

He removed her pants quickly, easily, and dispensed with his own while he stood above her, his chest moving hard and fast as he came down over her, his eyes glittering in his handsome face. But the separation was too much to bear. She pushed up on her elbows, her body lifting to find his, her eyes seeking, looking, hunting, her hands pulling for him.

There was no room for self-consciousness, no room for doubt, no room for worrying about how she'd feel in the morning. A fire was raging out of control and the only way to put it out was to indulge it completely. His hands on her thighs were strong, insistent, spreading her legs wider, his arousal poised to take her, and she held her breath, desire arcing inside her in a kind of mania.

Her nails scraped down his back, urging him forward, and he laughed gruffly, but it was a sound that was as deranged as she felt.

She bucked her hips as he thrust into her—and it was not a possession of slow, lazy intent; this was a sheer, blinding thrust of need, hard and desperate. He drove into her and she cried out because it was *everything* she'd ever thought she could want in life.

She tilted her head backwards and his stubbled jaw ran across her décolletage then lower, his mouth, warm and moist, curving around one of her nipples, his tongue lashing it until she was in a state of delirium. His hard arousal thrust into her again and again, his hands lifting her bottom, holding her higher so he could reach all of her, and then one hand was moving around to her womanhood, his fingers tormenting her most sensitive cluster of nerves until she was whimpering with the sheer agony of her desire.

'I feel like I'm on fire,' she groaned, and he smiled against her breast, but it was a smile of tension, because the same agonising want was throbbing through him, churning his gut, making him impatient for a release that he wanted to stave off as long as possible.

'I like being on fire,' she said, not even sure the words made any sense; her mind was no longer a part of her body. There was only this: feeling, pleasure, desperate yearning. He moved rhythmically, his body stoking hers, and she pushed up on her elbows as a tidal wave of need she couldn't fight, didn't want to fight, dragged at her and she let it pull her out to sea. It crashed against her, pleasure a rush of awakening that made breathing almost impossible.

She cried his name out, tasting it as she exploded in his arms, oblivious to the way he stilled, watching her, his eyes intent on her pleasure-creased face as she fell apart at the seams and slowly breathed herself back together again. He watched her and just as her breathing slowed he began to move again, so her eyes flared wide, locking to his, shock in them because her needs were already back, desire shifting inside her, greedily seeking more. He spoke to her in Greek, hushed words she neither recognised nor understood, words that filled her with pleasure just the same, words that were perfect in that moment, as he drove her to the heights of her pleasure anew.

This time, when the wave dragged her under, it dragged him with it, and she held onto him for dear life, as though everything she was depended on being close to him. They were adrift at sea, but adrift together.

Just that moment, just that night.

Alice stretched in bed, the silk sheets like gossamer against her well-kissed skin. She smiled at Thanos, not at all self-conscious in her naked state. How could she be? After they'd made love on the ottoman, he'd lifted her up and carried her to this sumptuous bedroom, laying her on the bed where he'd continued to pleasure and delight her body, kissing her most intimate flesh, tasting her, inviting her to explore his body, to look and learn, and she'd lost herself down the rabbit hole of sensual awakening, a hazy fog of lust pummelling her from the inside out.

It was now somewhere near dawn, but she wasn't tired. Not even a little. She lifted her fingertips to his chest, tracing a line down the centre, her eyes following the gesture lazily. He was bronzed all over. She liked looking at his skin. She liked looking at him.

'You know,' she said, pushing up on one elbow

so she could look at him properly, 'you're very, very good at that.'

Her fingers pushed lower, trailing the line of hair that arrowed down his abdomen.

'My ego is glad you think so.'

Her lips twisted in a half-smile.

'I didn't really know it could be so...*whoa*...'

'Whoa?' he teased, his eyes shuttered so she couldn't discern emotion in their depths.

'So mind-blowing,' she clarified, swirling her fingers in figures of eight, just below his navel.

'Ah.' He made a sound of comprehension, swiftly followed by a knitting together of his brows. 'And that's...different for you?'

His accent was thicker in this snatch of time, before daylight danced across the horizon, pulling out of the ocean's depths.

Alice's fingers moved lower, slowly, so slowly, until her fingertips brushed against the base of his erection. She felt his swift intake of breath and smiled at the raw rush of feminine power.

'I don't really have much experience.' Her eyes flicked upwards and now there *was* self-consciousness there. 'Definitely nothing compared to you.'

She didn't see the frown that etched across his face.

'You were not a virgin?'

'No.' Her smile was wistful. She wished, in

that moment, she had been. It was ridiculous, but the only thing that could have made what they'd shared more meaningful was if he'd been her first. She could make her peace with the fact this was a very temporary affair, she could make her peace with the fact that soon—in a matter of months—their marriage would be dissolved and they'd go their separate ways. But somehow, that didn't detract from the specialness and uniqueness of what they'd just shared.

'But you haven't found sex "mind-blowing" to date?'

She bit down on her lip, shaking her head. 'I mean, I was only with one guy.' Her eyes lifted to his. 'Once.'

He was very still then, and not because her fingers were continuing their exploration of his erection. 'You have only had sex *once* before?'

'Well, now I've had sex a lot,' she teased, sobering at his look of absolute disbelief.

'I know that must seem ridiculous to someone like you,' she said quietly. 'But it wasn't really…a great experience. Definitely not one I was rushing to repeat.'

Thanos reached beneath the sheets and captured her hand, pulling it away from his member with a warning look. 'I cannot think when you do that.'

'Good.' She blinked at him with mock innocence.

'I want you to explain to me,' he insisted, lifting her hand to his lips and pressing a kiss against her fingertips so her heart jolted inside her.

Alice sighed, her eyes shuttering a little, her gaze focussed on his lips. He was sort of like a conversational solar eclipse; there was such an intensity in his eyes that it was hard to concentrate when she looked directly at him.

'There's not really much to explain. I learned my lesson,' she said quietly.

'What lesson is that?'

She forced her eyes to his then, burnt sugar holding glowing amber. She aimed for lighthearted; it came out strangled. 'That handsome men who promise you the world aren't to be trusted.' She flicked her lips into a smile for good measure; Thanos didn't return it. Nor did he relinquish his hold on her gaze.

'It's funny. All my life my mom drummed it into me again and again that men weren't to be trusted.' Her smile was wistful. 'It wasn't her fault. My dad burned her pretty badly and we both had to live with the consequences of that for a long time.'

'What did he do?'

She shook her head. 'It's a long story. The point is, he broke her heart and she made sure I grew up knowing there's no such thing as Prince Charming or saccharine happy endings. She was trying to protect me, and I guess she really did have a point.'

He frowned; she didn't notice.

'But then I met Clinton, and despite being a walking cautionary tale, everything I knew to be true, everything Mom had always said, flew out of the window as I fell head over heels in love with his smooth lines.'

'He was your contemporary?'

'A few years older,' she corrected. 'Twenty—which to an impressionable sixteen-year-old meant the world.' She shook her head with disbelief. 'I was such an idiot.'

'You were sixteen?'

'And foolish.'

'What happened?'

She expelled a soft sigh. 'I slept with him and I thought it was the beginning of something amazing and special and incredible.'

'But it wasn't?'

She shook her head, her expression unknowingly haunted.

'So what?' His voice was impatient, but not with her. 'He what? Broke up with you once you'd slept together?'

Alice swept her eyes shut, the awful, horrible

fallout from that weekend something she tried to forget. 'More or less.'

'Meaning?'

'Oh, he was a bastard,' she groaned, blinking her gaze to Thanos's. 'He made sure all of his friends knew he'd been my first, that I was bad in bed, inexperienced.' She shook her head. 'I thought I loved him, and he… It was a pretty horrifying experience.'

'Men like that are overcompensating for some personal deficiency.' The words were snapped from his mouth, disapproval zinging around the room.

'Undoubtedly.'

'You are not bad in bed.'

It was so not what she'd expected him to say that Alice laughed, a soft sound, and when she looked at Thanos, she found him staring at her in a way that made her body tremble a little.

'Anyway, it was an eternity ago. I'm definitely not the same girl I was then.' She tilted her chin defiantly, remembering how true that was, the leaps and bounds she'd come on since then. 'He taught me a lesson that I shouldn't have needed to be taught, but it's one I've never forgotten.'

'And what lesson is that, Kyria Stathakis?'

Her lips pulled a little to the side. 'Not to be such a gullible fool.' The mood between them had shifted; there was an intensity between them and a vulnerability within her that she didn't entirely like. She pulled her hand away from him, teasing it down his body once more, her eyes holding a silent challenge as they connected to his.

'I wouldn't have slept with you tonight if it weren't for the fact we both know what the boundaries of this are.'

He didn't move; didn't speak.

'I like that you've been honest with me. I like that we both have our reasons for knowing this will run its course and we'll go our own way. I've learned not to trust anyone but, somehow, I do trust you, Thanos.' Her hands curved around his arousal and a throaty breath pushed out of him, lifting his chest.

Thanos wasn't sure he'd ever had anyone say those words to him. It did something completely foreign to his chest. 'Why?' The question was grated out of him, as his ability to think and process were lost in a fog of uncertainty.

'Because you're not making any promises.' She flicked her gaze to his and then pushed up at the same time she pulled the sheet off his body. 'You've been honest with me from the start, and the reason I know you're telling me the truth is because nothing you've said has been designed to get me into bed.'

She straddled his legs and brought her face closer to his arousal, her eyes holding his. 'I'm here because I want to be.' It was the last thing she said before she curved her lips over the tip of his arousal, and Thanos lost any ability whatsoever to speak, think or worry.

As dawn began to crest over the ocean, spreading light and newness into the valley of vines, Thanos pushed out of bed, taking a moment to look back at a sleeping Alice before pulling on some briefs.

Her eyelids moved frantically—a sign of deep sleep and busy dreams—and he smiled a little, wondering if he was in her dreams.

But his smile shifted from his face as he moved from the bedroom back into the lounge area, his eyes falling first to the ottoman, his body hardening as he remembered the frantic, animalistic passion of their coming together, the feeling of absolute, sheer need driving him to her as though everything he was depended on that possession.

But Thanos was no stranger to sexual passion. He liked women. He liked being with women. He made no apologies for his appetite, nor did he need to. Alice was right—Thanos never lied in order to seduce a woman. In fact, he was always at great pains to be blindingly honest with any woman he was interested in.

Thanos wasn't the kind of man to offer 'more'—the elusive promise of something beyond the physical. He had no interest in anything other than sex, and never had done. It was one of the reasons he generally kept his 'relationships' to a one-time affair. It was a lot harder to hurt someone if you only spent a night in each other's company.

And that had worked for him—it had been easy. Guilt-free.

But there was danger here, so much danger. Because everything was different with Alice. The intensity of his need for her was unlike anything he'd ever known. The sex had been mind-blowing, just as she'd said, so he'd been insatiable for her, wanting more and more and more. Even now, after knowing the pleasures of her body, her hands, her mouth all night, he was still filled with a hunger for her, a desperate craving that wouldn't quit.

But by far the biggest danger they faced was that he couldn't simply walk away from this. He couldn't kiss her on the lips and fly off in his helicopter, back into his real world. He couldn't turn his back on her and never see her again, as he ordinarily might.

She was his wife, and, even though they both knew their wedding was practicality at its finest, they were inescapably bound.

Sex complicated that. It complicated it in a way that meant he couldn't make his peace with it, and yet he already knew he couldn't walk away from it either. What he needed was to regain a sense of control; to put some boundaries in place. Because she was right. He hadn't lied to her, and he didn't intend to. Not with words, certainly, but not with actions either. He owed it to both of them to show he could control the passion that flared between them. It was a delight to be carefully enjoyed, not a need that should be allowed to overtake them.

He wouldn't allow it, and he was Thanos Stathakis so naturally he didn't, for one moment, doubt his chance of success.

CHAPTER EIGHT

'WHAT HAPPENED WITH your father?'

He lifted his gaze from the newspaper he was reading to find Alice watching him with undisguised curiosity.

The yacht had been a bad idea. A very bad idea. If he'd been wanting to prove to himself that he could control this flame of desire, suggesting they take his yacht out onto the Balearic Sea had been foolhardy in the extreme.

From the minute Alice had appeared in a floaty sundress with a huge wide-brimmed hat, he'd felt a pulsing of warmth in his body that had had less to do with admiration than it did amusement—a sentiment he feared was just as dangerous.

She'd brought a huge bag with her, packed with books of all things, and a big bottle of water, as though she didn't realise his yacht had a commercial-grade kitchen on board as well as an army of staff to keep them fed and serve them drinks of any variety.

But it was when she'd removed her sundress to reveal a bright red bikini that he'd known it was going to be harder than he'd banked on to control his need for her.

Alice Smart—no, Alice Stathakis—had the most tantalisingly creamy skin he'd ever seen. Flawless and pale, with golden undertones, and toes that had been painted a surprising black matte in colour. She'd wiggled them as she'd read, and he'd found the sight of that infuriatingly erotic.

He'd had to fight an urge to ask her what she was reading. To ask her if she read often. What her favourite books were. To ask her anything and everything. Because asking, he feared, would lead to knowing her better, and, more than that, it would lead to looking at her and wanting to strip that scrap of Lycra from her body and make love to her right here on the deck of his yacht, with not a care in the world for the possibility of drone cameras overhead or long lenses on shore.

'You don't have to talk about it if you don't want to,' she offered, an apologetic heat creeping into her cheeks.

He frowned, not perfectly able to recall what she'd asked.

'I guess it was pretty hard for you. Having him be sent away.' She turned back to her book, her dark hair plaited in a single braid, which she'd pulled over her shoulder. The tasselled ends landed against her breast; a breast he'd touched and tasted and was hungry to feel again now. Her skin would be sun-warmed and salty from the ocean.

'It wasn't hard.' The admission surprised them both. Him, because he rarely spoke of Dion Stathakis to anyone. Even he and Leonidas, by unspoken yet mutual consent, had formed a silence when it came to their father and his wrongdoing. Of course, Leonidas had so much more to resent the man for than Thanos did—Leonidas who had lost his wife and child in a madman's revenge against Dion. But Thanos had still lost enough to hate his father with all his soul.

'No?' She pressed a finger into the pages of her book and placed it on her lap. His eyes followed the gesture.

'I wish he'd received a life sentence. No, sometimes I've wished he'd been put to death.'

Her breath made an audible gasp as she processed this.

'You may think that's harsh,' he said softly. 'But you have to understand the damage he did, the life he took.'

'Whose life?'

Thanos let out a laugh—but not one of amusement. 'Mine, my brother's, my grandparents' legacy, and theirs before them.' He shook his head in disapproval. 'He ruined everything and not because he needed money, but because he wanted power. Not the kind of power you can have when you own half the hotels in Europe,' Thanos pointed out with a wry shift of his lips. 'He wanted people to fear him. He wanted them to tremble when he entered a room.'

Alice was quiet for a moment and Thanos wondered if she was regretting asking the question. But after a moment, she shifted her body weight, pushing onto her side so she could face him properly. And even in the midst of recounting a time in his past he loved to forget, his eyes were drawn to the sway of her breasts, and desire offered a very welcome reprieve from the darkness of his thoughts.

'Were you afraid of him?'

The question was not at all what he'd expected. 'No.'

Alice frowned. 'Did you know he was involved in the mob?'

'No.' His nostrils flared as he breathed out, and he reached a hand towards her, running his fingers over her plait, flicking the tail distractedly. 'I am not being intentionally vague.'

'I know that.' She grimaced. 'I guess it's not exactly your favourite topic.'

His eyes flew to hers, cinnamon clashing with burnt butter. 'I never speak about him.'

'I didn't mean to be invasive.'

He frowned, because, strangely, he hadn't felt

that she was. 'It's fine.' He flipped onto his back, staring at the sky. 'If we are to convince Kosta that I am a changed and happily married man, it's important we know each other well. We have no way of knowing what conversations will come up when we are at Kalatheros.'

He didn't see the small frown that crossed Alice's face, so couldn't have guessed the reason for it.

'I was not afraid of him, but nor did I feel affection for him. I suppose, if anything, I was wary of him.'

'Wary of your own father?'

Thanos nodded, a muscle jerking in his jaw. 'He was…erratic, at best. And I think he didn't like me, so what time we spent together was shaped by that dislike.'

'That would have been very hard to live with.'

He appreciated that she didn't try to argue with him. He could have imagined an outsider might have insisted that *of course* Dion had liked him. But Thanos was no fool, and his father's sentiments had been made abundantly clear over the years.

'I didn't particularly like him either,' Thanos quipped, in a futile attempt to lighten the mood. 'Leonidas—my half-brother—is only three months older. When my mother left me on Dion's doorstep, it heralded the end of my father's marriage.'

'Because you were…'

'Proof he'd cheated,' Thanos finished for Alice. 'Though I'm sure Leonidas's mother must have known even before I showed up. My mother was not the only mistress Dion spent time with.'

He looked at Alice in time to catch the sympathy in her expression. Strangely, he didn't resent it in the way he usually might. Thanos never welcomed sympathy or pity. Even as a child, he'd pushed back against those emotions.

'That's not your fault, though. How could he dislike you, because of it?'

Thanos let out a soft laugh. 'I was also a pretty unlovable child.'

Alice didn't laugh in response. 'How can you say that about yourself?'

'It's true. Even my own mother couldn't bear to be with me.'

'Why do you say that?'

'Because it is honest.' He reached a finger out, tracing the line of her lower lip. 'The last thing she said to me, before leaving me at Dion's—a man I didn't even know existed—was that she couldn't handle being my mother any more.'

Alice's sharp intake of breath did something to his gut. The wall of cement he kept locked in place to shield those memories from prying minds and fingers developed a crack. He welded over it, plastering a dismissive smile on his face.

'I was a handful. I don't blame her.'

'Well, I do!' she snapped. 'How could she say that to you? At eight years old!'

'I probably deserved it.'

Alice glared at him. 'No eight-year-old deserves that.'

'I was stubborn, sullen, demanding, and difficult.'

'So are all kids. In different measure, admittedly,' she said, a little frown forming on her face. 'But if she really felt like that, then there had to have been other options besides just depositing you with a father you didn't know you had.'

'It was a strange reality to find myself in,' he said truthfully, remembering that first afternoon, walking around the mansion, the servants' whispers filling his young ears, Leonidas's mother's shrieks burning them.

The knowledge, weeks later, that he was responsible for breaking up their family.

He turned away from her, his expression suddenly stony.

'Do you ever speak to her now?'

'No.'

'God.' Alice reached a hand out and curved her fingers over his forearm. 'That's a really awful thing to have gone through.'

He shrugged. 'I guess so. But you know what?'

'What?' Her voice was thick with emotion.

'It gave me Leonidas.' He turned to face her. 'I don't have much of a mom or a dad, but I have a brother who also happens to be my best friend. And I think sometimes the war zone we grew up in—parents who were always fighting, our dad going through a string of wives who were all destined to be disposed of within a year or two of the marriage—meant we grew even closer. You know?'

'Sure, like a shared trauma,' she agreed. 'I can definitely see that.'

'So when we realised the extent of his criminal activities, it was sort of easy to just emotionally detach from the mess he'd made. We cut him out of our lives and focussed on what really mattered.'

'Rebuilding your wealth?'

'The wealth, sure, but, more importantly, our grandfather's legacy. We spent a lot of time with him. He was the one who really raised us. We both felt we owed it to him to fix what our father had done.'

There was silence except for the gentle lapping of salt water against the side of the yacht.

'I think what you did is amazing.'

He jerked his gaze to hers.

'I mean it,' she insisted, perhaps intuiting his

surprise. 'To come out of the scandal and shock of what your father did, to put it behind you, to focus on making good from bad—that's not something everyone has the strength to do.'

'But you do,' he said, after a moment, making the connection easily.

'You think?'

'Sure. Look at how you're caring for your mom. You're a young woman who's put her mother ahead of everything else, who's doing all that is good and right because you love her. What's that if not layering good over bad?'

Alice shook her head softly. 'What else could I do?'

'You've given up just about everything for her.'

'She gave up everything for me.'

'How so?'

Alice gnawed on her lip. He lifted a thumb and padded it over her lip, so she stopped, her eyes huge when they met his. 'We were really poor.' Her cheeks flushed with pink as she made the admission and he wondered, for a moment, if she was embarrassed to admit that to him. 'And Mom was incredibly bright. She should have had a dream career before her, but instead she got pregnant with me and had to work really hard just to keep her head above water.'

'What about your father?'

Alice closed her book, placing it on the deck

beside her. The sunshine bounced off the cover, making it sparkle.

'I never knew him.'

'They weren't married?'

'No.'

'And he wasn't in your life?'

'Not at all.'

Thanos frowned, wondering if this was why she hadn't questioned his assertion that Dion simply hadn't liked him. She understood, apparently better than most, that the bonds of parenthood didn't necessarily guarantee love and loyalty of the life-laying-down variety. Unless... 'Is he dead?'

Her smile was genuinely amused. 'No. You think a guy has to be dead to be a deadbeat dad?'

'Of course not.'

Alice sighed softly, her breath brushing his temples, so he felt a kick of desire that almost overwhelmed him with an urge to act on it.

'My mother was only nineteen when she met him. She thought they were in love. He seduced her, promised her the world, slept with her and then vanished into thin air.' She cleared her throat. 'It's part of the reason I couldn't believe I'd been so stupid with Clinton, you know? I was so determined I wouldn't become my mother and then I walked right into the exact same situation. It's almost like all her warning me off men somehow tempted fate and led me right to the same kind of douche who'd broken her heart.'

Thanos nodded thoughtfully. 'There are some men out there who get a kick out of hurting women.'

She shrugged. 'I don't know if that's what it was with either of them. Clinton was immature and, yes, he did hurt me. But my father was so much worse. He made a calculated and determined effort to seduce my mom. He really did promise her so much, and he fought for her to fall in love with him. He set out to hurt her, I think.'

'Why?'

'I don't know. Sport? A game? Power? I can't fathom it. But it's irrefutable that he went out of his way to make her love him and then vanished.'

Thanos frowned. 'When she discovered she was pregnant, did she contact him?'

'Yeah.' Alice's voice was hoarse. 'Even then, she wanted to believe it had all been some kind of mistake, that he'd been called away on urgent family business or something. She loved him. She thought it was a dream come true.'

Alice reached her hand out, grabbing the soda that was at her side, and took a sip, replacing it with a little frown on her pink lips. 'He did everything he could to evade her, and when she finally caught up with him, she discovered he was engaged to someone else. Her world came crashing down around her that afternoon.'

'And she told you this?'

'She told me enough. She wanted to warn me off men like my father.' Alice's grimace was loaded with grief. 'And to warn me off men in general, I think. My mother, once bitten, was definitely twice shy. She couldn't even accept that, while my father had been an out-and-out cheat, there might be a man out there who would love her and accept her and do everything he could not to hurt her.'

Thanos lifted a brow, his eyes skimming Alice's face thoughtfully.

'What?'

'Nothing.' He shook his head.

'I'm serious. What?'

And despite the tone of their conversation, a little laugh escaped him. 'It's just...do you think either you or I are in a position to judge her for that?'

Alice regarded him inquisitively.

'You don't think you push men away because you're traumatised by what she went through? And what you then went through with Clinton?'

Alice's expression tightened. 'No.'

'Alice.' He reached a hand out, lacing his fingers through hers. 'That's not a criticism.'

'Isn't it?'

'No. I happen to think pushing people away is an excellent life choice.' His voice was layered with light sarcasm. 'I only mean it's understandable that your mother didn't feel like she wanted to jump back into dating someone after all of that.'

Alice was quiet, but the column of her throat shifted as she swallowed. 'She also worked. A lot. We were pretty broke, so she had to work long hours and I don't think a love life really fit into that.' She expelled a soft, impatient breath. 'The thing is, when you said you hated your dad, I understood. I understand. Because I hate mine, even though I've never met him.' She fixed him with a steady stare, her eyes swirling with ice. 'I've made my peace with the fact he didn't want to be a parent. That he never wanted to know me.' The husk of her voice, though, betrayed her—she hadn't really made her peace with it.

Who could?

'But he's a wealthy man, Thanos. I know because I looked into him, when I was old enough to do a search on the Internet. He's wealthy and married with other children. I have no idea how many women he treated as he did my mother, but I do know he was in a position to help us and he never did.'

Thanos's eyes glittered in his handsome face and he was, temporarily, at a loss for words.

'She wrote to him, begging for some kind of financial assistance. When I was eleven, I earned a place at a prestigious selection school. It was a scholarship but didn't cover the cost of boarding and uniforms—which were out of Mom's reach. She wrote to him. He flat out refused.'

Anger shot through Thanos. 'How could he refuse? Surely there was some legal obligation, setting aside his obvious moral obligation.'

Her eyes were awash with memory, as though she'd been sucked back in time. 'No. He's British, and the American courts couldn't enforce anything. Despite the fact he's incredibly wealthy, he had no interest in helping my mom with frivolities such as, you know, food, let alone a private education for me. Besides, she couldn't really afford a good lawyer, so…' Her voice trailed off.

'She did try to get him to at least contribute something.' Alice shrugged as though it hadn't mattered. 'But he sent nothing except lawyer's letters, all of which took more money to respond to.'

Thanos stared at her, no idea what he could say to make this better.

'I hate him,' she said simply.

Thanos's eyes showed his own feelings quite clearly. 'So do I.'

And at that Alice laughed, and it was as if the sun were bursting out from behind a storm cloud.

Everything tilted a little, shifting and reshaping, and Thanos's breath burned in his lungs as he stared at her and wondered how the hell he hadn't noticed how beautiful she was the first moment he saw her. How come it had taken him days to recognise the danger here? To see not only that she was attractive, but also that he was obsessively attracted to her?

He'd already spent more time with her than he ever had with a woman he was sleeping with. Shared more of himself. Cared more for her stories.

But he didn't panic—too much. Because he was controlling this; he had rules and boundaries, and every intention of abiding by them.

'Tell me about this bikini,' he said, his tone completely different, lighter, teasing, a relief from the emotional heaviness of their previous conversation.

'What would you like to know about it?'

'A great many things, Kyria Stathakis,' he drawled slowly.

Did you buy it with me in mind?

The question was on the tip of his tongue but it created an impression of dependence he didn't wish to encourage, so he pushed it aside.

Alice, though, shifted her attention to her body, her cheeks heating pink, as though she was just realising that she was practically naked beside him.

'I had no idea what I would need for this…job,' she said quietly.

'Job?'

'Our marriage.' She lifted her fingers to mime inverted commas, which shouldn't have bothered Thanos at all. It certainly shouldn't have made him feel a rolling of nausea in his gut.

'I mean, this is *so* far outside of my wheel-house,' she said with a self-deprecating laugh, gesturing around the boat. 'I live in suits at work and yoga pants at home.' Her shoulders lifted in a shrug. 'And I wanted to fit in. To make this seem realistic.'

'You do fit in.'

She pulled a face. 'Only because I did my re-search.'

'Research?'

'Uh-huh. And Kosta was right about one thing, Thanos. There are a *lot* of pictures of you on the Internet.'

Something inside Thanos tightened painfully over his chest, like a metal arm being pressed hard to his sides.

'So?' The word came out harsher than he'd intended.

Alice didn't appear to notice. 'I needed to see how your usual, um, friends…' her cheeks heated pink and he wondered how he hadn't realised her degree of inexperience earlier '…dressed. The kinds of clothes they wore. This bikini seemed pretty standard.'

Thanos stared at her, unable to pinpoint why he was so annoyed at that revelation, unable to explain why he felt frustrated and…something else. Only that her casually delivered explanation filled him with a sense of being weighted down.

When he didn't speak, Alice grew quiet and a lift of his eyes to her face showed that she was anxious now. 'Is it…okay?'

More frustration. It roared through him. He was being a self-obsessed idiot. She'd done the right thing. She'd approached this marriage with professionalism, just as he would have expected. This was a marriage conceived of for one purpose, and the better she played her part, the more likely it was to succeed.

'It's perfect,' he assured her, his voice throaty, his eyes clouded with the intensity of his thoughts.

'So what else were you wondering?' she prompted, her eyes lightly teasing now.

His body hardened, and he pushed every thought from his mind with great care, acting purely on instinct as he stared at her intently. 'Just how easy it is to remove.'

She smiled sweetly as she stood, straddling him, her legs on either side of his body, her head blotting out the sun.

'Pull on the string, and find out for yourself.'

CHAPTER NINE

'KALIMÉRA, KYRIA STATHAKIS.'

The words, spoken in his native tongue, were like little beads of sunshine rolling over her skin. Alice stretched, muscles that were not used to being so well used flexing in her body. She stifled a yawn, shifting a little in the enormous bed. Beyond the window, the vines of France were a heady, vibrant green. She shifted to face him, wondering at what point they'd decided she'd join him in his room, rather than keeping to the terms of their agreement—that she would have her own space; that they'd hardly see each other. In fact, in the five days since their wedding, they'd barely been apart.

Alice might have found that troublesome, except for the certainty that their essential terms weren't changing. So they'd blurred the lines a little. So what? That was just wiggle room. Lots of wiggle room.

Neither of them was being silly about this. They both knew there were divorce papers signed in a lawyer's drawer somewhere, waiting for Thanos to make the call to have them filed.

She shifted a little, her gaze lifting to his handsome face.

'I like it when you speak Greek.'

He arched a brow. '*Tóte tha to káno sychná.* Then I will do it often.'

She smiled and placed her head flat against his chest once more, her fingertips chasing invisible circles over his taut flesh.

'I could teach you.'

'Greek?'

'Mmm.' She heard the agreement rumble through his chest.

'I'm already learning Italian.'

The fingers exploring her spine stilled. 'Are you?'

'*Sì. Ma non posso parlare bene.* But I can't speak it very well. *E molto difficile.*'

'Why are you studying Italian?' he asked in that tongue.

It took Alice a moment to put her answer into the right words. 'So that I can speak like a native when I go there.'

His hand began to move up and down her spine once more. 'You want to go to Italy?' He was back to English.

'*Sì,*' she said, a wistful smile on her lips.

'Italy's beautiful, but it is no Greece.'

Alice laughed softly. 'And you wouldn't be at all biased?'

He shrugged, the action dislodging her head a little so she lifted her face to his, pressing her chin into his chest. 'You will decide for yourself when we go there.' His hand lifted to her hair, running through it, curling behind her head. 'Why Italy?'

The past pulled at her like a string attached to her soul that she could never snip.

'Beyond the fact it's meant to be one of the most beautiful places on earth?'

'Yes.'

She smothered a smile, knowing he wouldn't let it go now he'd decided he was interested.

'For a year, we lived in Massachusetts. Mom got a job working in a call centre for a phone company and she had a friend with a spare room so we packed up and moved.' The description neatly glossed over how hard that time had been in Alice's life. She'd been twelve, and had started to put down roots, to make tentative, hesitant friendships that she'd bitterly resented having to leave.

'It was cold and dark and I hated it,' Alice said with a wry smile. 'To be fair to Massachusetts, I was a miserable pre-teen determined to hate the world and everyone in it. I'm pretty sure my perception was altered by that veil.'

'You were a miserable pre-teen?' he said with obvious disbelief.

Alice nodded sagely. 'Oh, yes. I was an *excellent* adolescent.' She shook her head then reached for his hand, lacing her fingers through it distractedly—and as though it were the most natural thing in the world.

'We had a neighbour, Signora Verde. She used to see me come home from school and I guess she worried about me—Mom worked late and the friend of hers we were living with was a nurse who had shifts all sorts of hours. I was home alone a lot. Signora Verde would bring me plates of *biscotti* and hazelnut *bomboloni* fresh from the stove. She'd sit with me a while, and tell me about her town in Tuscany—Trefiumi Nord.'

Alice shook her head wistfully, remembering Signora Verde so clearly. 'The way she described it…a hue of autumn colours all year round, walls that were golden and ochre with red-tiled roofs, buildings that nestled close together along streets that were ancient, lined with little uneven stones, roads that curved gently uphill, perfect for little Vespas to scoot along, window boxes overflowing with fragrant flowers—their pops of colour in the summer enough to take your breath away. The sound of old women sitting on plastic seats by their front doors, talking about their grandchildren as though each was a *maestro* in the making. The smell of garlic thick in the air, the noise of children running, clutching *gelato* in their sun-bronzed hands.' Alice's stomach clenched with the same sense of longing she'd felt then.

'Signor Verde got transferred to North Dakota about six months after we moved to Massachusetts. I never saw her again. But the memories of Italy formed a part of me, and, no matter how hard things got, no matter how hungry I felt, I always remembered three things because of Signora Verde.'

'And these things are?'

Alice smiled, with no idea of how the morning light caught in her eyes and turned them to pools of liquid gold—nor the effect this had on her husband. 'That Italy is heaven on earth,' she said with a wink. 'That kindness—when you expect nothing in return—is the most important gift you can give anyone.' The words were whispered because, truly, Signora Verde had come into Alice's life at a time when her heart had been heavy and she had been so full of angst and sadness, a displaced, angry teenager.

'And the third?' His question was heavy with feeling.

'The taste of freshly cooked *bomboloni* on a frigid winter's afternoon.' She smiled up at him, and her tummy rumbled on cue.

Thanos laughed. 'I can see Greece has a lot to live up to.'

'It does.' She looked towards the window, the ocean glistening in the distant background.

Thanos's smile was distracted and he was quiet for a moment. 'Would you like to go to Italy today, Alice?'

She laughed, shaking her head. 'You can't be serious?'

'Why not? Italy is only a two-hour flight. We could go for lunch.'

Alice laughed at the very idea. 'And then what? Paris for dinner?'

'If you'd like.' He shrugged, but Alice's heart turned over in her chest at the image he was painting. It was all too much. Even with all the evidence to the contrary, she found it almost impossible to believe this was her life—albeit temporarily.

'Thanos.' She laughed again, pushing up so she could see him more clearly. 'You can't just suggest we get on your private jet and fly to Italy for *lunch*!'

'Why not?'

'Because it's… I mean…it's just so…'

'Yes?'

What? So exactly what she wanted? So completely as if her dreams were coming true?

'So perfect,' she said seriously now, her eyes

filling unexpectedly with moisture. 'Thank you. I'd like that. A lot.'

His smile released a thousand butterflies in her tummy.

'So, Alice? Which would you prefer? Venice, Rome, or Florence?'

She weighed those choices and then shrugged. 'Surprise me.'

His grin was relaxed. '*Tóte as páme*. Then, let's go.'

Her heart turned over in her chest as she pushed out of bed. The sun was shining on a brand-new day and Alice was going to Italy. For the first time in a very long time, Alice felt truly, utterly happy.

In the end, they went to none of the cities of Italy. Alice described Signora Verde's town Trefiumi Nord to Thanos and, with a little Internet searching on the flight over, they touched down in Florence and slipped into a limousine at the base of the aeroplane. Local time was an hour behind Port D'Angelo.

'How far away is it?' she asked, leaning forward and looking out of the window.

'Not far. Half an hour.'

Alice bit down on her lip, excitement coursing through her veins. She couldn't believe she was here in Italy—the place she'd wanted to go all her life.

And because of the man beside her.

'It's beautiful,' she murmured to herself as the car sliced through the countryside. Enormous pine trees formed a forest over rolling green hills to the left of the car, and to the right gentle undulations in a patchwork of yellows gave way to a distant view of a stone castle.

As the car drove nearer to the castle, it came alongside a bubbling river, which glistened in the early afternoon sun.

'Another river.' She pointed to a fast-flowing body of water, crossing the first at a right angle.

Beside her, Thanos nodded. 'Trefiumi Nord literally means Three Rivers to the North. I imagine the town is named for this.'

Alice turned to face him, her eyes sparkling, a smile on her lips.

'I think Signora Verde said something along those lines.' She sat back in the seat, contenting herself with watching the vista as it scrolled past their windows, with no concept of how Thanos watched her, his dark-rimmed eyes roaming over her face, seeing every flicker of delight, every roll of excitement.

'Thanos, look!' she squealed, as the car rounded a bend and a small town appeared almost out of nowhere. Nestled in the base of several rolling hills, it was crammed full of yellow and golden terracotta homes, a castle in the centre with a renaissance church and cupola beside it, pencil pines poking up between some of the homes.

'Oh, Thanos.' She spun to face him. Alice was alive—and breathtaking. 'I had no idea it would be even prettier than I'd imagined.'

The car drew to a stop on a narrow, cobbled street, and Thanos's chauffeur, Ryan, was there, opening the door. Alice stepped out, emotions flooding her as she breathed in the fragrance and atmosphere of the place—a place which had always lived in her imagination but which was now a part of her reality.

'Thank you. For bringing me here.'

His eyes were heavy on her face, his expression impossible to interpret. 'You are very beautiful when you're excited.'

An instinctive habit of knocking away the compliment filled her but she ignored it. When Thanos looked at her, she *felt* beautiful, and it had very little to do with looks.

'*Grazie,*' she whispered softly, smiling up at him.

They stood like that for a moment and to all the world, to any outsider, they must have looked like a perfectly normal pair of newlyweds. Completely besotted, in love, enamoured of one another.

Which was just as well, because a flash went off a moment later with an audible 'click' sound of a cell-phone camera.

Alice turned in that direction to find a woman holding her phone towards them. At being recognised, the cell-phone photographer quickly spun and walked away.

Alice frowned. 'Did she just take our photo?'

Thanos's expression was grim. 'It happens.'

'You're serious? People actually just…take your picture?'

He nodded, putting a hand in the small of Alice's back and guiding her away from the limousine. 'Let's keep moving.'

Alice went with him, but she couldn't get the invasiveness of the press in his life out of her mind. 'That really happens to you?' she asked with a small shake of her head.

He tilted a wry smile at her. 'I am somewhat recognisable.'

Alice stopped walking and looked up at him, frowning. True. Thanos Stathakis was instantly identifiable—not least because he was frequently in the tabloids. The idea of living such an exposed life didn't sit well with her.

'You must hate that.'

He considered that for a moment. 'I don't particularly enjoy it.'

They weaved through a narrow street with cobbles underfoot and as they walked Thanos reached down and took Alice's hand in his and she didn't even question it. The intimacy felt normal. She liked the way it felt to hold his hand, their fingers weaved together, his thumb lightly stroking the back of her hand.

Alice couldn't take her eyes off the streetscape. It was everything Signora Verde had described, and more. The residents were vivid in her imagination and the reality was just like it. The smells, the sounds, the tiny little boutiques—clothing shops, book stores, restaurants, cafes, it was all so quintessentially Italian, she felt as if she'd stepped onto the set of a movie.

'Here.' Thanos slowed as they approached a pair of ancient timber doors nestled at the base of a stone building. Alice paused, looking up, running her eyes over the place.

The sign above the door read Ristorante Vecchio Città.

'Old City Restaurant?'

Thanos grinned. 'You're fluent already.'

Alice laughed. 'Barely. I've got a long way to go.'

'Do you take lessons?'

'No, I couldn't afford that, and I don't have the

time.' She didn't see the way Thanos's expression darkened. 'I use free apps. They're good. They keep me distracted on the subway.'

He guided her towards the doors, which, on their approach, were opened inwards by an older man with silver-grey hair and dark black eyes. He was tall and wiry and wore a black apron with white stripes over a crisp white shirt and black pants.

'*Signor.*' He nodded curtly, gesturing into the restaurant. 'Welcome.'

'Thank you. We'd like a table for two. Something with a view.'

'Of course.' The waiter nodded and his eyes seemed to linger on Thanos for a few seconds—moments in which Alice surmised he recognised the billionaire tycoon, because within seconds the best table in the restaurant was made available and a bottle of champagne brought over, compliments of the house.

Alice took the seat offered, so distracted by the view that for a moment she said nothing. From the street it had been impossible to identify this building's location but she saw now it was right on the edge of one of the three rivers that ran through the heart of this town. A little way down there was what looked to be a medieval bridge, like a miniature version of the Ponte Vecchio, with shops built along either side of it and fairy lights strung across the roof.

The water ran quickly and children were sitting at its edge, one holding a fishing line, the other reading a book. In the distance, a family sat on a blanket, drinking wine and eating sandwiches.

It was idyllic and breathtaking.

The champagne was poured and they were left in peace with a menu that was all in Italian.

'What do you feel like eating?' Thanos asked.

She scanned the menu, picking out the words she could recognise.

'What do you think looks good?'

'Would you like me to translate?'

She nodded. 'I can read some of it.'

'Show me what you recognise.'

She lifted her eyes to his, a hint of embarrassment in her expression. 'Really only the simple ones. Bread, chicken, ham, pizza, pasta.'

'That's half the menu,' he pointed out with a grin.

Emboldened, she focussed her gaze on the words and slowed it down. '*Carne*…meat…with green beans. Potatoes.'

'*Perfetto,*' he complimented.

Her heart warmed. 'Truffle *fettucine*.'

'You know more than you think.'

Pride swelled inside her. 'Thank you.'

'*Piacere.*'

The waiter returned. 'My wife will order,' Thanos said with an encouraging nod of his head.

'What would you like?' she whispered.

He reached across and pointed to the steak on the menu.

Alice, in halting Italian, with the server waiting patiently, listed a few dishes. The waiter asked questions, speaking slowly, and Alice gave the full force of her concentration to him, so she didn't see the way Thanos was regarding her, his expression a mix of admiration and pleasure.

When the ordering was done, and the waiter had disappeared, Alice's cheeks were glowing pink with happiness.

'Wow. I think he actually understood me.'

Thanos nodded. 'You spoke well, and have a good accent.'

More pleasure. 'I'm not sure about that. But it's my first time attempting to use my Italian with a native speaker.'

'I think if you spent more time here, you'd be fluent in no time.'

'Maybe.' She sipped her champagne, the bubbles popping against the sides of her mouth. 'How many languages do you speak?'

He considered that a moment. 'Greek, English and Italian fluently, passable French and German, conversational Spanish and Cantonese.'

Alice's jaw dropped. 'Whoa.'

'Whoa?'

'Yeah. How did you learn? I'm struggling just to become passably good at Italian.'

He shrugged. 'I had the advantage of travelling, often, living in many of these places. And our piano teacher was Chinese—an exceptional musician with barely any English, so we learned how to speak casually with her.'

'I'm impressed.'

'Languages are just communication, and communication is inherent to all people.'

She sipped her champagne, considering that. 'It must make your business easier, that you can communicate all over the world.'

He dipped his head in silent concession.

He was an incredibly intelligent man, focussed, dedicated, successful. That took a fire and aptitude that was incredibly rare. Yet he was renowned for being a playboy, a party animal, someone who was more comfortable with a glass of Scotch in his hand than a billion-dollar business deal in his grip.

Alice ran her fingertip around the rim of her champagne glass, lost in thought, and a moment later, the waiter appeared with plates of food.

'I got it right,' she joked, as exactly what she'd ordered appeared. 'I was half worried ox tongue might appear.'

Thanos's wink was purely friendly, but it fired

desire deep in her gut, and suddenly she didn't particularly feel like eating, she wanted to be alone with him, somewhere with a bed and a lockable door.

The food was sublime. Traditional Italian, rustic, fresh, flavoursome, and Alice found herself wishing she hadn't lost contact with Signora Verde, so she could tell her that she'd been here, that she'd eaten on the edge of one of the rivers that wended its way through Trefiumi Nord.

'When you are distracted, you get a lovely little line right here,' he murmured, reaching across the table and running a finger between her eyebrows.

Alice made an effort to straighten her face. 'I'm not distracted.'

'No?'

She pulled a face, her heart pulling as though caught on the end of a fishing line when she contemplated how well he suddenly knew her. 'It's just...'

'Yes?' he prompted, when her words trailed off into nothingness.

'You're not at all like what I would have thought.'

He set his fork down, leaning back in his chair, carefully watchful. 'No?'

She shook her head. 'You have this reputation as the playboy prince of Europe.'

He shrugged and she knew she wasn't imagining a defensive tightening of his features. 'Apparently.'

'But you're not… I don't know. I can't really see that.'

'Why not?'

'Well, you're fiercely focussed, for one.'

His lips lifted in what was almost a smile. 'You think that precludes me from enjoying an active social life?'

She pursed her lips. 'No. But I don't think you do *enjoy* that kind of lifestyle. It doesn't gel.'

'Gel?' He repeated the colloquialism with a small tug of his lips.

'Suit you.'

'Ah.' He kept his eyes on hers as he sipped his drink.

'I'm serious. I just can't imagine you going from this—' she waved her hand towards him '—to some kind of bachelor on a yacht surrounded by drunk supermodels.'

He didn't smile. His expression was unreadable.

'It got me wondering about which version of you is real?'

He expelled a breath, turning to look out of the windows. 'Can't they both be real?'

She frowned. 'I don't think so.' Alice leaned forward on the table a little, her heart running a bit faster. Despite the intimacies they'd shared, she wondered if she'd overstepped the mark in some way.

'It doesn't matter,' she offered quietly, when several moments passed without him speaking.

'I'm not ignoring you,' he said, finally. 'I was just trying to frame an answer.'

Her stomach flipped.

'I like the noise that a lot of people together make.'

And despite the seriousness of their conversation, a small laugh escaped her. 'That's your answer?'

His owns lips twisted in a smile. 'I don't know. It's hard to explain, I suppose.'

Alice thought about this. 'I've never liked crowds, myself. Nor parties. I find that kind of shallow social interaction so meaningless. Making conversation with someone you don't really know, who you don't care to know.' She studied him thoughtfully. 'I suppose parties are a great way to surround yourself with people without really forging deep relationships.'

Thanos was very still, watching her. 'Do you think that is what I do?'

The little line formed between Alice's brows. 'I don't know. What do you think?'

He expelled a breath, a grim set to his jaw. *'Forse,'* he responded—perhaps, in Italian. 'Parties became a habit some time in my teens. It grew to be a way of life I didn't question.'

She sipped her champagne, surprised to see the glass was almost empty. A waiter appeared almost instantly, topping it up. 'And now?'

He waited for her to expand.

'When you've bought P & A, and our divorce gets filed?' The words lined the insides of her mouth with acid. She swallowed to clear it. 'Will I see your photo in the tabloids again, a different woman by your side every night?'

Thanos's angular face was very still. 'Would that bother you?' The air around them was like mud; so thick, so stymying.

Alice dipped her eyes forward, shielding them from his inquisitive attention.

'It's not my business,' she pointed out slowly. 'We both know this is temporary. What you do when our marriage is over is up to you. I'm only asking if you still feel a pull towards that lifestyle.'

'We've only been married a week,' he pointed out.

Alice lifted her eyes to his, seeking something in the depths of his eyes. 'Yes,' she heard herself agree. 'It's only been a week.'

A week or a year, it didn't much matter to Alice. Something had shifted inside her, pieces of her soul were changing shape and morphing into something else, something unrecognisable.

Confusion was threatening to pull her into a dark vortex, so she pushed the thoughts aside and plastered an over-bright smile to her face. 'The calamari looks delicious.' She speared a piece and forced herself not to think of anything beyond this moment. Who or what he became beyond their marriage wasn't her concern—there was a reason she didn't want to think about it.

'In the cave?'

'Yes, and on the island.' He waved his hand around the wide space. 'We had many homes, but this was our favourite.'

'I can see why,' Alice said, sincerely.

'She grew up in the slums of Barcelona. She'd never seen anywhere so open and untamed.'

He blinked, as if clearing the memory. 'There are rock pools down there.' He nodded towards the other side of the cave, where a clearing gave way to another set of steps. 'You might enjoy a swim.'

'Definitely,' Alice agreed, lifting her face to Thanos's and startling silently. Because the man beside her was Thanos Stathakis—her pretend husband—but he was now, also, the formidable businessman tycoon, and she felt his determination emanating from him in tidal waves.

And in that moment, his worries were hers, his desires hers, and she wanted to do everything she could to help him get whatever he wanted in life. She wanted him to have P & A.

And impressing Kosta with how completely she'd changed Thanos was part of that, so she sucked in a breath and swore to herself she would play this part to absolute perfection—and that they wouldn't leave until Thanos had peace of mind about his company's future.

When they returned to the mansion, Alice faked a yawn. Thanos's eyes shifted to her face.

'Excuse me.' She smiled apologetically. 'I'm a little worn out. Do you mind if I have a rest?'

'Of course.' Kosta nodded, calling for a servant to show Alice to the room that would be hers and Thanos's. She slipped away from them, glad that Kosta and Thanos would have a chance to be alone together, knowing that all Thanos needed was a little time to bring the older man around to selling the property.

Alice woke to a feather-light touch on the tip of her nose. She lifted her hand to bat away what she thought must be a bug or a stray hair, and connected instead with Thanos's finger. Alice's eyes blinked open, a ready smile on her face. She was disoriented though, looking towards the window to see that the sun was lower in the sky, the day's brightness fading into evening.

'I fell asleep.'

Thanos grinned. 'Apparently.'

She lifted her hand to his chest, not questioning the easy intimacy that had developed between them. 'How did your afternoon go? Did you talk to him?'

Thanos made a noise of agreement.

'And?' She sat up in the bed so her eyes were level with his. 'Did he agree to sell it to you?'

Thanos's laugh was throaty. 'You are as impatient as I am.'

Impatient? Alice wasn't. In fact, there was a part of her that hoped Kosta would stretch this out, making Thanos take months and months to convince him, months and months of pretending to be married, just like this.

'He's close,' Thanos agreed, shifting his head forward a little, his eyes locked to hers as he brushed her lips. It was such a small gesture, and it reminded Alice of the night in front of the club, the night she'd agreed to marry him, but it was different too, because now he was familiar and she knew that the kiss could and would lead to so much more.

'We have an hour before dinner,' he said, his lips hovering just above hers.

'An hour?' Her eyes were heavy; she dropped them, breathing in as she pushed her body forward. A teasing smile flickered over her lips. 'That sounds like just enough time for a swim in those rock pools.'

'Exactly what I had in mind,' Thanos joked, as he found the bottom of her shirt and lifted it over her head.

His fingers moved with urgency, trailing over her body, finding her breasts, teasing her nipples, plucking them between his thumb and forefinger, his kiss deepening as he pushed her back against the bed, so every fibre of her being was vibrating with this total, desperate, all-consuming rushing of desire.

'I'm going to miss this,' he groaned, the throwaway comment said without thought, without meaning, but it drove a stake into Alice, splintering her pleasure for a moment, making it almost impossible for her to set aside the pain and feel only pleasure.

But then his mouth claimed one of her nipples and he shifted a hand to between her legs, his fingertips tormenting the sensitive cluster of nerves there, so she was totally lost to thought and feeling and was simply existing for this, for him, and for whatever it was their marriage had become.

CHAPTER ELEVEN

THANOS MEANT WHAT he'd said. He was going to miss this. He was going to miss Alice. The realisation landed against his side with a thud and he did everything he could to vanquish the thought. Casual sex was nothing new to him.

He was the playboy prince of Europe, wasn't he?

He dragged his mouth lower down her body as his hands removed her underpants, his tongue tormenting her flat stomach before finding the hair at the apex of her thighs, delighting in her responsiveness, her little sounds of pleasure that broke through the room.

He would never tire of this. Her body was like an instrument and he wanted to be its maestro. Anger soared in him whenever he thought of the man she'd once loved, who'd made her care for him, made her trust him, and had taken her virginity then discarded Alice as though she meant nothing.

Hypocrite, a little voice inside him whispered, as he brought his hands to her thighs, spreading her legs wider, allowing him greater access. Her hands threaded through his hair, her movements urgent, her heavy, impassioned voice begging him not to stop.

He didn't intend to.

But he wasn't a hypocrite. He was nothing like Clinton, who'd hurt her. Clinton who'd promised her the world and turned his back on her.

Thanos hadn't promised Alice anything. He'd been very careful about that. He'd purposely made sure he was painstakingly honest with her every step of the way. They'd slept together out of mutual need—both had wanted this, and both had agreed to it, knowing their marriage would end one day and this would all be over.

Over.

He didn't much want to think about that.

He kicked out of his clothes, then brought his mouth back to her womanhood, savouring the sounds she made as she moved closer and closer to climax, her body writhing on the bed, her hands digging through his hair faster, her desperation and insanity palpable. Right as she tipped over the edge, her orgasm claiming her, he brought his body higher up hers and thrust inside her, feeling her wet muscles contract almost painfully around his arousal, feeling all of her wrap around him until he was completely in her hands, utterly under her control.

But he wasn't ready to end this—he wanted more of Alice, more of this. They had time, and, for as long as they did, he was going to make the absolute most of every single second.

'You remind me a little of us,' Kosta said, a glass of Scotch in his hand, his long legs sprawled in front of him.

Two days ago, they'd arrived at Kosta's house, and he'd been an acquaintance to her then. But after a weekend in his company, exploring his home, wandering the beaches he'd enjoyed for most of his life, she felt a growing affinity to the man. She liked him.

'Of Helen and me,' he explained. 'We were like you and Thanos, you know.'

'Were you?' Alice prompted, sipping her own ice-cold glass of wine in an attempt to wash a hint of guilt from her mouth. She didn't much like lying to Kosta, now that she knew him. The only saving grace was that the end justified the means. Kosta wanted to sell P & A and she had no question that Thanos was absolutely the best person to take it over.

'We met and married within one month. The second I saw her, I knew I could not live without her.'

It was just how her mother had described meeting Alice's father in all those letters. And it hadn't worked out for Jane, because Henry Jennings had been a lying bastard. But love existed, love at first sight was real, and Kosta was living proof of that.

'When did she…?'

Kosta grimaced. 'Five years ago.' He shook his head, turning to look towards the ocean. The moon shone a silvery line down its centre, broken occasionally by the rolling waves. 'It was quick. Death, that is, not grief, not mourning. That I will do for the rest of my life.'

Alice's features were loaded with sympathy. 'I'm sorry. You don't have children?'

Kosta's smile was nostalgic. 'We had a son. He died when he was four. My wife could not fall pregnant again.'

Tears filled Alice's eyes. She blinked to dispel them. 'What a tragedy.'

'Yes.' His own eyes showed emotion. He lifted his Scotch to his lips, sipping it slowly, his fingers trembling a little as he replaced it on the tabletop.

'My business is a family legacy. I have no one to leave it to. No one who will carry it on in my name.'

Alice lifted her gaze to Thanos unconsciously. His expression was unreadable. 'I want to sell it, but not because I need the money.' He waved a hand around them, showing the terrace, and the beautiful home beyond it. 'I need to sell it so I can see it go to someone who will treat it as I do.

Who will value it as a family business, who will build it and pass it to their children and their children, as my grandparents intended.'

She swallowed past the lump in her throat. 'You know Thanos is the right man, don't you?'

He turned to face her, studying her intently. 'You love him?'

The question floored Alice. She knew what she needed to say, because she was playing the part of the doting, loving wife, but the question still had the power to detonate a bomb right beneath her ribcage. 'I...of course.' She jerked her head to cover the stutter.

'I can see that you do,' Kosta said quietly. 'And I hope he will make you happy. For many years I have wondered if he was capable of making anyone happy, himself included.'

Something like alarm was drumming against Alice's chest. 'Why do you say that?'

'I knew Nicholas—his grandfather—quite well. And through him, I met Thanos, when he first came to live with Dion.' He shook his head sadly.

Curiosity spurted inside Alice. 'Did you?'

'Oh, yes. He was a troubled child, driven by emotion, and I think quite insecure.'

Alice frowned, this description pulling on all her heart strings, even as she felt a desire to contradict it. Thanos wasn't insecure. Was he?

'You cannot blame him for that,' Kosta continued. 'His mother broke his heart, and his *father* was not worthy of that word.' He spat that indictment with obvious disgust. 'After the trial, Thanos began to spiral out of control,' Kosta continued, shaking his head.

Alice's heart squeezed tight. 'In what way?'

'Partying, drinking, anger. Leonidas held him together, just, but Thanos was on a dangerous downward trajectory.'

Alice wanted to do something, to say something. She clutched her own glass tighter, wondering why she couldn't simply reach back through time and make everything okay for the scared little boy Thanos had once been.

'I bought Petó because I truly believed Thanos would destroy it if he remained at the helm.'

This was news to Alice. She jerked her face to Kosta's to find him watching her shrewdly. 'I knew what it meant to him, what it had meant to my friend. I wanted to safeguard it from Thanos's ability to obliterate it.'

Alice let out a little noise, a murmur, of sympathy.

'You think that was wrong of me?'

Alice frowned so a divot formed between her brows. 'I can't say.'

'I like him,' Kosta surprised her by offering. 'I always have. When he came to live with Dion, I remember feeling disbelief and rage—rage that a man like Dion Stathakis could be awarded two such fine sons when...' He grimaced. 'He had two fine sons, and he appreciated neither. He wanted neither.'

Alice frowned, pity shifting inside her. 'He sounds like a fool.'

Kosta laughed, a crackly sound. 'Yes, and then some.'

'Thanos isn't like you think,' she said, after a moment. 'He won't do anything to hurt Petó, or P & A. In fact, I think he's the best person to run both.'

Kosta's eyes were on hers, a dark grey gaze loaded with intelligence. 'I don't worry he'll hurt the company. I worry he'll hurt himself. His lifestyle...' Kosta shook his head slowly from side to side. 'I understand how tempting it is to run from yourself. When our son died...' his fingers dug into the arms of the seat, as though it would somehow alleviate the pain '... I drank solidly for at least a year. Numbing myself—or trying to.' He fixed her with an intense gaze. 'But Helen saved me. Just like you have saved Thanos.'

Alice stared out at the water that surrounded Statherá Prásino, a serious expression on her pretty features. One of Thanos's yachts bobbed in the distance, immaculate and enormous, and—

she knew from experience—staffed with a small army, all ready to take the boat out on Thanos's whim.

In the two days since they'd returned from Kosta's home, a sense of uneasiness had followed Alice everywhere. She couldn't understand it, but she was waking up in the middle of the night with a curdling feeling of dread, the likes of which she hadn't known since Thanos had taken away her every single stress. She was no longer worried about bankruptcy or how she was to pay the rent, her credit cards were clear as a whistle, and her mother was in one of the top facilities in the world.

So why did she have a sudden and intense sense of foreboding?

She looked over her shoulder, scanning the lounge area. It was empty. Thanos was working.

The day was warm, though, the water inviting, and suddenly Alice craved the freedom of lying on her back in the sea, staring at the sky, imagining herself to be truly weightless.

She didn't bother to grab a towel or to change into her bathers. It was a private beach, a private island and she knew she'd dry off again by the time she reached the house. Something was driving her, pushing her to the ocean. At its edge, she stripped out of her dress, standing in only the designer briefs and bra that had been part of the wardrobe she'd bought to prepare for being Thanos's wife. Of course, she'd had no idea when she'd bought them that he'd ever see them. She hadn't even imagined that it might become physical between them.

She waded into the water, closing her eyes as she felt its salty balm against her sides, going deep enough to flip onto her back, just as she'd wanted, and stare up at the sky.

It was the perfect shade of blue, like something out of a fantasy. She lay on her back, breathing in and out, staying afloat as long as she could before she twisted onto her stomach and began paddling to shore. Her eyes scanned the house on autopilot, the enormous mansion so beautiful and breathtaking, and perfectly situated.

Alice hadn't been able to imagine what her life would be like, married to Thanos. If she'd tried to imagine it, she wouldn't have foreseen anything like the reality had been. And she struggled now to imagine her life in a post-Thanos world.

She'd have money, financial security, certainty for her mother's healthcare for the rest of her life. But no Thanos.

A gulf opened in her chest, as wide and expansive as the ocean she was swimming in. She tried to imagine waking up without him in bed, going to sleep on her own, not sharing a meal with him, not talking to him, not laughing with him, and the panic was back, gripping her tighter.

Because she was about to be completely and utterly alone.

But more alone than before, because for a brief while she'd known companionship and compatibility and it was all about to be stripped away from her.

Alice straightened her spine as she emerged from the water. She'd fallen in love with Clinton a long time ago, and he'd hurt her. He'd broken her heart, yet she'd recovered. She'd moved beyond it.

Whatever she was feeling now, she'd be able to beat that, too, when the time came. And until then, she was going to just enjoy being with Thanos, not dwell on a future that loomed, uncertain and all kinds of wrong.

Her fingers were toying with the necklace, sliding the diamond from side to side, a little line between her brows, the frown line he'd seen a lot these last few days. Something had shifted between them, at Kosta's place. He couldn't say what, only he felt an air of seriousness, of urgency, when they touched and kissed. He felt a sense of desperation, and he didn't know if it was coming from Alice or from him.

He had precisely zero experience with women to know what he could say to make her smile again. At least, not beyond one night. One night, he was fine with. But this kind of thing—something longer, something more meaningful—just didn't suit him.

And it *was* meaningful with Alice. He'd expected he could marry her, and even sleep with her, and somehow still abide by his usual behaviour with women, but nothing about Alice was like what he'd experienced before.

But that didn't change the fact that this thing was running its course. Not just because they'd agreed it would, but because Thanos had no hope of knowing how to maintain a relationship.

There was a reason he'd always avoided anything like commitment.

He was terrible at it.

And he didn't see a need to change that aspect of his personality. Still, he didn't like seeing Alice frown.

'You're going to break the chain,' he said, aiming for teasing and light-hearted. Her fingers immediately snapped away from it, her features apologetic.

'I didn't realise I was doing it.'

He bit back an impatient sigh. 'It doesn't matter.'

The stars of the night sky sparkled brightly, the isolation of his island ensuring complete clarity in the atmosphere.

'Kosta said something interesting about you,' she said slowly, her eyes roaming his face as though whatever it was might have an answer in his features.

'Did he?'

She sipped her wine, perhaps buying time. 'He said you were on a dangerous downward spiral, after your father's conviction.'

Thanos felt as if a knife were being sliced along the side of his heart. 'Oh?'

She nodded, somewhat self-consciously. 'He said your brother held you together.'

Thanos's smile was a self-deprecating acknowledgement of this. 'I think Kosta was right.'

'You're very close to him?'

'To Kosta?' Thanos joked, deliberately misunderstanding, looking for a smile any way he could get it.

She offered him a half-hearted lift of her lips.

'Leo and I were pretty much raised as twins from the time I came to live with him.'

'He didn't resent you?'

Thanos's lips were a grim line in his face. 'Perhaps.'

'I don't mean he should have,' she said quietly, reaching out and putting her hand over Thanos's, her comfort and perceptiveness qualities that made something sharpen against his insides. 'Only that he was a young boy himself, and his world must also have felt a bit like a bomb had been exploded into it.'

'I'm sure.'

Alice bit down on her lower lip. 'But you're close now?'

'Yes.' He smiled, because he wanted her to smile back at him, and she did, so his stomach rolled and all his breath threatened to explode from his lungs. Her smile was every bit as beautiful as the stars overhead.

'He seemed nice,' Alice said. 'And I liked his wife.'

'Hannah? She has been good for him.'

Alice was quiet a moment. 'In what way?'

'You know his first wife died?'

Alice nodded. She'd read about it at the time, and had heard of it again once she'd started temping at Stathakis. Murdered, along with Leonidas's son Brax, in a vendetta against Dion and his criminal connections. A shiver ran down Alice's spine.

'Leonidas closed himself off after that. He just took himself out of life; he became a shadow of his usual self. It was hard to watch.'

'But understandable,' Alice murmured.

'Perhaps at first. But after four years, I was worried he would never wake up again.'

'And she woke him up?'

Thanos's smile was spontaneous. 'Yes. She fell

pregnant—unexpectedly—and Leonidas had no choice. If he wanted to be a part of their baby's life, he had to open himself up to Hannah.'

'Their little girl looked adorable.'

'She is.' His smile turned to something more serious as he studied Alice's face. 'I cannot imagine what was going through your father's mind, to choose not to be a part of your life.'

Alice shook her head. 'Nor yours.'

'But I was a nightmare,' he said, his voice light-hearted despite his pronouncement. 'And you were, I'm sure, a delight.'

She pulled a face. 'Hardly.' Then she leaned forward, so her legs brushed his beneath the table and her fingers could lace through his. 'And you don't really think there's any justification for choosing not to be a part of your child's life, do you?'

His eyes glittered but he didn't answer.

'I came to accept, a long time ago, that my father was a person lacking in moral fibre. That his choices weren't a reflection on me. You must see the same is true of you and Dion?'

'I think I was not an easy child to love,' he said carefully, no longer wishing to continue the conversation. He pulled his hand away with an apologetic smile, and lifted his drink. He angled his face towards the ocean, wondering at the way his heart was slamming hard against his ribcage.

'I'm sorry you feel that way.'

He shrugged. 'Don't be. I became used to being completely alone in the world a long time ago. I like being alone, Alice. It's how I'm meant to be.'

CHAPTER TWELVE

WHEN ALICE WOKE with a start that night, she knew exactly why. The panic attack that was roaring through her was intense and impossible to ignore. A fine bead of perspiration had broken out on her brow, and her breathing was ragged. She shifted a little, casting a glance over Thanos before pushing the covers back and slipping from the bed. The silk negligee she wore moulded to her skin as she moved from their bedroom, down the wide, curving staircase and into the kitchen.

It was the middle of the night, the witching hour, when dark thoughts were at their zenith and hope seemed to have ceased to exist. The view through the kitchen windows was all black, save for a milky line of moonlight that trembled across the ocean.

'I like being alone, Alice.'

His words had woken her. They'd been rushing through her, jamming her sleep, blocking her dreams, filling her with a sense of desperation, because they were *wrong*. They had to be.

He'd chosen to be alone to protect himself, and more than anyone she understood that. She'd done the same thing, hadn't she? Sure, she'd moved around a lot, but choosing not to make friends was a way of staving off hurt. Loss was something Alice had seen as a way of life, a necessity, and so she'd closed herself off to any hope of happiness and friendship.

The one time she'd let herself believe that maybe there was someone out there who would choose to love her, she'd been forcibly reminded of how completely unlikely that seemed.

So she'd gone back to choosing solitude, loneliness, and a lack not just of companionship, but of everything.

She'd fallen into a track of being on her own and it had taken this sham marriage to pull her out of it, to realise how incredible it felt to let yourself share with someone, to be vulnerable with them, to enjoy their company and crave more of it.

Her heart gave a funny thump and she sat down on one of the kitchen stools with a little gasp of understanding.

Because she hadn't just come to rely on Thanos.

She'd come to think of him as a part of her, or maybe that she was a part of him. Just that they were wound together, woven as if made of cloth, and no divorce could dissolve that. And this marriage wasn't the reason this had happened. It was something much bigger and more important than that.

She'd fallen in love with him.

She loved him.

She loved him in a way that made her unable to bear the thought of leaving him. She loved him in a way that made it impossible for her to think that he might not feel the same way—that he might be anxiously waiting on Kosta to sell P &A so he could walk away from this.

Worse, to get back to the life he'd led before they'd met.

At that, a genuine wave of nausea exploded inside her, the idea of seeing him with another woman, of seeing him with some glamorous model or actress draped over his frame, was as painful to her as if she'd cut off a limb.

She loved him. The more she thought about it, the more it exploded in her brain, the realisation as clear and plain as day. Why hadn't she seen it earlier? It was in every single moment they'd shared. She definitely hadn't realised it at the time, but from the first meal they'd shared—in that incredible restaurant tucked away in New York—something had been happening inside her. Something huge and powerful and all-important.

She had to tell him.

But what if he didn't love her? What if he didn't feel the same way?

Uncertainty shimmered on the edges of her brain because she knew from experience that there was every possibility of that.

Her own father hadn't loved her.

And Clinton had walked away from her—had derided her and humiliated her.

What if Thanos did the same?

Oh, he'd never hurt her, she knew that, but what if he looked at her with sympathy swirling in the depths of his beautiful eyes and shook his head, explained that he simply didn't love her? That she was living in a fantasy world to even *hope* he might?

Then she'd live.

Somehow.

She'd coped with heartbreak before. True, never like this had the potential to be, but it had been bad. Soul-destroying. Ugly. Unpleasant. And yet, she'd coped then; she'd cope again.

What she'd never make her peace with was pretending she didn't feel the way she did—pretending she didn't feel as though her heart were going to burst from inside her chest, to explode all the way through her.

She could live with loss.

But never, ever with not knowing.

* * *

'Thanos. Are you awake?'

He flung an arm over his eyes, squinting into the complete blackness of their bedroom. When had it become 'theirs'? He didn't even frown as the word slipped through his mind.

It was just for now. He could deal with that.

'No.'

She made an impatient noise and then Alice's fingers were prodding him in the shoulder. 'I'm serious. I need to speak to you.'

He wanted to go back to sleep. He'd never needed much—a few hours a night—but those few hours he generally liked to sleep deeply and undisturbed. Still, there was something in Alice's tone that penetrated his fog, so he sat up, his eyes scanning her face.

'Is something wrong?'

'No. Yes.' She let out a tremulous laugh. 'I don't know.'

His expression shifted, worry slipped inside him. 'What is it, *agape*?'

The column of her throat shifted visibly as she swallowed. 'I… I couldn't sleep.'

He laughed. 'So you thought you'd wake me to suffer in insomnia with you?'

She bit down on her lower lip and it wasn't light enough to see her properly, so Thanos reached out and switched on the bedside lamp.

Both squinted a little as they adjusted to the brightness.

'I need to speak to you.'

'Okay.' The word was a prompt, an invitation.

But Alice didn't speak. She seemed to be choosing her words carefully, but she also seemed to be anxious about something. Stressed. Nervous.

He hadn't seen her like this since that first day in the office when she'd been staring at the stack of overdue bills and her face had been ashen and her eyes bleak.

'Tell me,' he prompted, knowing that whatever it was, he'd fix it. Money, health, her mother? 'Alice?' Impatience zipped through him. Still, she didn't speak. 'I can't help you if I don't know.'

'I'm trying,' she said, her eyes beseeching.

But it wasn't good enough. Concern was slashing through him as a whip would butter. 'Try harder.'

Her voice shook when she spoke. 'What are we doing?'

It wasn't at all what he'd expected her to say. 'Huh?'

'This. You, me.' She pointed from him to her. 'What is this?'

Something shifted inside him, an emotion he couldn't quite grasp. Guilt. Annoyance. Frustration. 'I don't understand.' His voice was guarded.

She breathed out softly, shifting a clump of her dark brown hair so he reached a hand out and caught it, smoothing it behind her ear.

'This. Our marriage. I—can't make sense of it.'

He placed his hand on her arm, gently stroking her smooth flesh. Goosebumps trailed in the wake of his touch. 'What's to make sense of?' he prompted, trying to join the dots and unable to connect them. He looked around for his phone, to check the time.

'Alice, it's two in the morning. Three hours ago we were making love and now you look as though you've seen ten ghosts. What's happened?'

A strangled noise erupted from her chest, a pained noise, and his worry grew.

'I couldn't sleep.'

'You said that.'

She nodded jerkily, standing then, pacing towards the window and staring out of it. She wore a flimsy silk negligee and even then he ached to draw her into his arms, to pull her to his body and pleasure away whatever was worrying her.

'I keep having this premonition of disaster,' she said. 'Like a blade of panic that comes out of nowhere. And I had no idea why; I couldn't understand it because everything's so good. Perfect, actually.'

She turned around to look at him, her expression haunted, her eyes pleading.

'And this is a problem?'

She nodded slowly, her expression stricken. 'Yeah, I think it might be.'

His laugh was just a short, sharp sound of confusion. 'Why?'

'Because it's the kind of perfect I want to hold onto.' She bit down on her lip, allowing her words to sink in. 'It's the kind of perfect I want to last for ever.'

For ever. Her words slammed into him, and on a cellular level he rejected each one instantly. There was no such thing as for ever. No such thing as happily-ever-after and a perfection that didn't disappear.

'I fell in love with you, Thanos.' Her voice cracked, and then there was silence, as if she was waiting for him to speak. But he couldn't because panic was strangling him, just as she'd described, wrapping around him, making his eyes a little blurry, and his brain squeal.

'I didn't mean to.' Now she was whispering, wrapping her arms around her torso so she looked both ethereally beautiful and fragile all at once. 'I swore I wouldn't ever get involved with a guy again. I was done with men.' The words were laced with self-directed anger. 'And then you came along and you were so different.'

She drew in a shaking breath. 'Different from

anyone I've ever met and so different from what I expected.'

She crossed to where he sat—mute, and like stone—and kneeled before him. She had no choice—it was the only way to meet his eyes.

'I couldn't work out why I've been experiencing this growing sense of unease, but then when you said last night that you like being alone, that it's how you're meant to be, it made me see everything clearly. I don't want to be alone.' She shook her head. 'I mean, I don't want to be with anyone else either. I want to be with you.'

It was like grating his feet on boiling bitumen. He shook his head in a silent, visceral rejection of her words. He could imagine a future just as she painted it, with no end point on this marriage, with Alice by his side day in, day out, for no purpose other than that they enjoyed being together, and, damn, so much of him wanted to agree, to admit this had changed completely from what he'd expected, too.

But the thing was, there was *always* an end point. To every relationship in life, there was a cessation, and he'd rather know when and why than be blindsided. He needed those boundaries in place.

His eyes met hers and pain opened up inside him, because he felt her upset, he felt it pulling at him.

'Alice.' He had to think of what to say. She stared at him, almost as though she were holding her breath. 'What do you want from me?'

She opened her mouth, apparently not sure of that. 'I want to know how you feel.'

'How I feel?' His response was unintentionally scathing.

'Yes.' Her eyes sparked with courage. 'Because I don't think I'm the only one who's been falling in love here.'

He ground his teeth together, rejecting her implication whole-heartedly. Love was a minefield he had no intention of getting involved with.

The very idea filled him with the sense he was falling off the edge of a very tall building.

'Not once—' he spoke slowly, clearly, choosing his words with great care '—have I given you any reason to think love was on offer.'

He heard her shocked intake of breath and, a second later, tears sparkled on her lashes, tears that might as well have been made of acid, being dripped onto his flesh. 'You don't think?'

'I know. I have been very careful on that score.'

'Liar,' she whispered, her own anger obvious now.

'From the beginning, we have both been absolutely clear about the parameters of this.'

'We said one thing,' she muttered, 'and did another.'

His heart careened into his ribcage as he acknowledged that there was potentially some truth in that.

He'd been careless and stupid. His own rule of thumb—of never getting involved with anyone—had served him well all his life. And the one time he'd let his guard down, he ended up in this mess.

And it was a total mess. Because he didn't want Alice to be upset. He didn't want her to be hurt. And he sure as hell didn't want her to go, and he had a sneaking suspicion that she would, if he didn't play his cards very, very carefully.

'I like being with you.' His voice was gentle. 'Isn't that enough?'

Her eyes lifted to his and she was quiet, which he took as a very encouraging sign. Carefully, he continued. 'You think you're in love with me.' He ignored the way her eyes narrowed and her lips tightened. 'But I think maybe it's just sexual infatuation. This has been pretty amazing.' He smiled, to show how much he meant that. 'I think that we should just keep going as we are. Enjoy what we have. But not get too invested in what comes next.'

The second she stood, he knew he'd said the wrong thing. She hadn't been listening with an open mind, she'd been listening with obvious disbelief.

'What comes next is already here.' She bit down on her lip and he had the most awful feeling that she was trying not to cry. 'I don't "think" I'm in love with you. I know I am. And knowing that, there's no way I can keep pretending to be your wife, making love with you—' her voice cracked '—if it doesn't mean anything to you.'

He stood up, rejecting those words, pulling her into his arms. 'I didn't say it means nothing,' he growled, the words almost primal, coming from somewhere deep inside him. 'I just don't want you to think sex equates to love.'

'It's not just sex,' she said, not facing him, pressing her cheek to his chest. 'It's everything I feel when we're together. At dinner. Waking up beside you. I love you. I love your mind, your ideas, your passion, your determination. I'm head over heels in love with every single part of you and it will suffocate me if I have to stay here with you pretending I don't feel that way, or knowing that you don't feel that for me—I can't do it. I just can't.'

He groaned, stepping back from her just enough to see her face. He pressed a finger beneath her chin, tilting her face up to his. 'So what do you want?'

She opened her mouth, her eyes laced with disbelief, and every cell in his body was compelling him to say something, to beg her to stay anyway, to promise her just enough to keep her with him. Hell, to lie to her, if that was what it took.

But he couldn't do that.

He couldn't say he loved her when he didn't.

He felt as if he was losing his mind; nothing made sense.

'I want to go home.' Her voice was hoarse. 'I know we had a deal. I can try to pay you back what you've already spent on Mom. It will take me time but I can—'

'Seriously,' he interrupted, staying completely still. 'Don't. You think I care about *money*?'

She jerked her face away from his. 'I think you're paying me a lot of money for a marriage that I'm walking out of.'

'You did your part,' he muttered, dragging a hand through his hair. 'You saw Kosta, so, as far as I'm concerned, your obligations to me are at an end.'

She swept her eyes shut for a moment. 'Then there's no reason for me to stay here.'

He was eight years old again, having the rug pulled out from under him, having all the boundaries of his world shift brightly and unexpectedly. He was eight years old and losing someone important and valuable and unique in his life. Except this was different, because he was making this decision; he was in control, just like always.

The thought didn't reassure him at all.

But there was no way he could offer Alice what she needed—no way he'd even try. He knew what she'd been through with Clinton; he wasn't going to be another asshole who broke her heart.

'I'm sorry,' he said, simply. 'I was careless with you. I should have guarded against this better.'

A tear rolled down her cheek and his gut clenched hard and fast.

He didn't touch her. He no longer felt he had any right.

She swallowed, her face so pale, so pinched. 'What next?'

The question caught him by surprise and, briefly, hope flared in his chest, because that sounded like there was the opening to change her mind.

'I can't get off the island without you,' she whispered.

Logistics.

Ice trickled down his spine. Damn it, he didn't want her to get off the island.

He jerked his head once more. 'Do you want to stay the night?' Hope was back, his body crying out for just one last time, one last night holding her, breathing her in, one more morning of waking up with her in his arms.

She shook her head, fear in her expression, and he realised she was drowning in panic and heartbreak—because of him—and he couldn't fix this. The one thing that would make it all better wasn't in his power to give.

Desperation gnawed at him.

All he could do was to make this smoother and easier. He had to help her leave, had to stop fighting, stop thinking about what he wanted and help her get home. Help her forget him.

The insides of his gut clenched.

'I'll fly you to my hotel in Athens,' he said firmly, not a hint of emotion in the words. 'You'll stay the rest of the night in a room there, and in the morning, if you still feel you want to return to America, my plane will take you.'

She nodded, blinking away from him. 'Thank you.'

Thank you?

For what?

Thanos Stathakis felt like just about the worst human on the face of the planet. He sure as hell didn't deserve her thanks.

CHAPTER THIRTEEN

'SHE'S DOING WELL.'

Alice looked up at the nurse without hearing what she'd said.

'Your mother. She's looking well.'

Alice turned back to Jane Smart, looking at her through fresh eyes. It was true. She looked much better than she had in a long time. The facility was state-of-the-art, but it offered incredible extras. Every day, Jane was wheeled into a beautiful garden, custom-designed for comatose patients. 'The latest research suggests many of our patients are still capable of absorbing external stimuli—sunshine, warmth, a light breeze, the sound of birds chirping,' the director of the hospital had explained. 'Besides, it can't do any harm.'

Alice had smiled and nodded, acted as she'd thought she should act, when really she felt exactly as she had done in the two months since leaving Stathera Prásino.

Like a ghost, living a half-life, going through the motions instead of actually feeling anything.

She had been wrong on the island. Wrong the night she'd told Thanos how she felt. Wrong in a thousand and one ways.

Wrong to tell him how she felt, because nothing could have been worse than this. Continuing to be with him, even knowing she loved him and he didn't love her, would have been preferable to this never-ending state of loss.

She'd been wrong to think she'd get over this. Wrong to think this pain was on any playing field even remotely near what she'd felt when Clinton had humiliated her. Even the lifelong knowledge that her father had no interest in her paled in comparison to the all-consuming sense of absolute grief that stalked her daily.

Daily?

Every minute.

It had been two months.

Two months since they'd flown in complete silence over the Aegean, down low into Athens. Two months since he'd accompanied her into his six-star hotel, arranged for a penthouse suite, escorted her to the door, wheeling the luxury suitcase that was stuffed with designer clothes, two months since he'd stood back as she'd pushed open the door and prepared to walk away from him.

He'd kicked his toe in, leaving the door ajar, his eyes holding hers. 'If you change your mind,' he'd said quietly, letting the implication fade away.

But she'd known she would never act on that. Even if she did—which she had, many times— change her mind, and decide she would take any pain for the promise of a few more nights of Thanos.

The one thing she was glad for, and proud of, was that she'd stayed strong. She'd returned to New York, and, only a week or so later, had dropped her wedding ring and the enormous necklace into his lawyer's office, needing any souvenir of their marriage to disappear.

He hadn't acknowledged that, but the following week she'd received the title deed and keys to a place on the Upper East Side. When she'd caught a cab to look at it, she'd felt as if she were living in some kind of macabre fairy tale.

It was beyond anything she could ever imagine. An enormous four-bedroom apartment with two separate living spaces, decorated and furnished in a manner that would please a queen, with a pool on the wide terrace that boasted sensational views over Central Park in one direction and the city in another.

She hadn't stayed there yet.

She couldn't bring herself to.

Not without knowing if it had once been Thanos's. Or if he'd bought it with her in mind. Neither option was okay. Neither option made her feel good.

'I think she likes the sunshine.' The nurse was still talking.

Alice dropped back into the present with a thud, pasting a weak smile on her face.

'She always did.' Tears filled her eyes, but they were tears for Thanos, for Jane, for Alice, for her dad, tears that had come so easily since she'd left Greece.

'I'll leave you alone,' the nurse said softly, excusing herself with a little squeeze of Alice's shoulder.

She nodded, and when she was alone, she put a hand on her mom's. 'You got through it,' Alice whispered. 'I wish I knew how.'

And she wondered then if it would have felt different, if she'd had a child.

Thanos's baby. The very idea made her groan, because having just a piece of him would have kept love warm in her heart, would have filled her with something, at least, to focus on.

But then what?

Would he have insisted they stay married? And she'd have been trapped in a marriage with a man who didn't love her, who couldn't love anyone, who would no doubt come to resent her?

She groaned again, and put her head on her mom's hand, closing her eyes. She breathed in, and told herself it would be okay, even when she really suspected it wouldn't be.

She went to see her mother every day. She needed routine and rhythm, something to do that might distract her, and seeing her mom at least reminded her that she wasn't entirely alone in the world.

Two months became three.

She still felt no better, but surely one day that would come?

'You said it was just for show,' Leonidas said quietly, looking around Thanos's office with an expression of disbelief.

And Thanos could see why.

The space that was usually kept immaculately ordered more closely resembled a pigsty.

'It was.'

Pséftis,' Leonidas drawled. 'If it was just for show, you wouldn't be existing on alcohol and coffee three months after she walked out on you.'

'I have told you a thousand times,' Thanos snapped harshly, reaching for his Scotch glass— which was disappointingly empty, 'she didn't walk out on me. We came to a mutual decision that it was time to end the sham of our marriage. It served its purpose. Kosta is having papers drawn up even now, as we speak.'

Leonidas nodded, his eyes glinting as he studied his brother. 'Yes? So why are you not celebrating?'

'How do you know I'm not?'

Leonidas laughed, a sharp sound of rejection. 'You are wallowing. It is the exact opposite.'

Thanos ground his teeth together, reaching for his Scotch decanter and refilling the glass. He held the bottle towards Leonidas, who curled his lips in a derisive negative.

'Do you know what I think of, when I look at Isabella?' Leonidas asked urgently, moving a step closer to his brother's desk.

'What?' A snarl.

'I think about what a responsibility it is to be a parent, to be a father. I think about our childhoods, about the way our father let us down time and time again. I think about the way my parents fought constantly, so I knew only acrimony in relationships. I think about the fact I almost let Hannah—the best thing to ever happen to me—walk away because I had no idea how to love someone.' He lowered his voice, calming his tone a little. 'I think about you, and how it must have felt to have your mother literally give up on you.'

Thanos's spine stiffened and he took a glug of Scotch, wincing as it hit his palate.

'I think about how impossible that should

be—to turn your back on your own child. The idea of never seeing Isabella again makes my body ache all over.' He shook his head. 'Your mother deserted you, she chose not to love you, and you have spent the rest of your life feeling unlovable.'

Thanos finished his Scotch and stared into the empty glass, wanting everyone to go away, wanting to be alone. Particularly, not wanting to hear these words.

'You live with a chip on your shoulder the size of this island because it's easier than accepting your mother failed you and your father failed you and that you deserved better. They failed you, but now you're taking it one step further and failing yourself.'

Thanos ground his teeth together. 'You don't know what you're talking about.'

'You love her, don't you?'

Thanos glared at his brother with a rising phoenix of white-hot fury. 'For the last time, no! I don't! I don't love her, okay!' And he threw the Scotch glass across the room, until it landed with a burst against the wall and shattered into a thousand tiny shards.

'You're screwing everything up,' Leonidas said, with the kind of honesty only a sibling could offer.

'Oh, go to hell.'

* * *

Thanos hadn't had a drink in two weeks but he sure as hell could have used one. He sat opposite Kosta on the deck he would always remember from the last visit, when he had sat beside Alice, his arm around her shoulders, her body curved into his side, her fragrance, her sweetness, her willingness to help him in this ruse setting him on fire. Now he sat on the deck in a thoroughly different mindset, in a thoroughly different mood. Even the weather was different. The sky was grey today, clouds low, so the ocean was moody and unimpressed.

'I'm sorry Alice could not be here today,' Kosta murmured.

Did Thanos imagine the way the older man's eyes shifted a little, sympathy swirling in their depths?

'The contracts are ready?' Thanos barrelled past the statement, beyond caring that he was being rude.

Kosta nodded slowly.

'She's not well?'

Someone, somewhere, had offered this small lie to Kosta, when the trip was being prepared. Perhaps his assistant? He didn't know.

Kosta shifted his gaze out to the murky sea, his expression grim.

She's not well?

It was such a simple enquiry, and Thanos had no way of answering. Was Alice well? Was she happy? His chest ached as if he'd been punched.

He had no way of knowing.

They didn't speak, they didn't communicate at all. He couldn't have even said if she was still in America.

Despair groaned through him, as it often had these past three and a half months.

The whole idea had been stupid.

Pretend to be married to buy a company he was paying more than market value for from a man who was desperate to sell. Thanos should never have indulged in such a childish game. It had been foolish, foolish, foolish.

And for the first time in over a decade, he no longer cared if he reacquired Petó. It was not the most important thing in his mind or heart. In fact, the acquisition felt trivial and banal.

'She left me,' he said instead, turning back to Kosta. 'We only got married to fool you.'

Kosta didn't react for several seconds and Thanos dropped his head, running his fingers through his hair.

'At the time, I thought I wanted Petó badly enough to do anything to get it.'

Kosta remained silent and watchful, in a way that unnerved Thanos because it reminded him so strongly of his grandfather.

'It seemed easy enough,' Thanos continued. 'You wanted me to settle down, so I did. Or at least pretended to.'

'You didn't change your lifestyle?'

Thanos shook his head. 'That's not what I meant.'

'So you are still making being a bachelor a championship sport?'

Thanos locked his jaw.

'Because I have not seen you in the papers once since your marriage.'

Thanos swallowed. The idea of living the way he had before Alice was something he couldn't contemplate. He shook his head. 'I'm not here to discuss my marriage.'

'Your marriage only existed because of my ultimatum,' Kosta pointed out shrewdly. 'You think I don't have a right to understand?'

'There's nothing to understand. It's over. It was all a lie.'

Kosta shook his head slowly, his features laced with pity. 'No, it wasn't.'

'You don't know what you're talking about.'

'I know more than most.' He leaned forward a little. 'Thanos?'

He lifted his head.

'I like you.'

Thanos grimaced, feeling somehow even worse than he had before. Because Kosta was a good and kind person to whom Thanos had wilfully lied. What the hell had come over him?

'I have always liked you, more than I let on. Your grandfather told me a story about you, once. We were at a party in Europe and a princess was there. She made a speech, remarking on how her son had built the most amazing tower out of Lego. It was two feet high, she said, with windows and a door, turrets that climbed inches higher. Nicholas leaned towards me, a proud smile on his face, and told me that you'd decided, one summer, to create a house using rocks from down near the beach. According to him, you went down every day with a canvas bag, loaded it up and returned to the garden, where you set to work. It took you months, but, rock by rock, you did it. I didn't really believe it at the time—grandfathers exaggerate, in my experience—but a year or so later, I went to his island and there it was, still standing, this small house you'd made, all because you'd set your mind to it.'

Thanos remembered. He remembered the weight of the rocks, the feeling of the sun baking his back, the cuts on his hands as he locked each piece into position.

He ground his teeth together. 'What's your point?'

'I knew then that you were a young man who

would achieve whatever he wanted in life. You have a rare talent that disposes you to success. When you form an intention, there is nothing that will get in your way. I knew what I was doing the day I told you I wouldn't sell you P & A unless you settled down.'

Thanos had the distinctly unpleasant feeling he was being manipulated.

'You knew? That it wasn't real?'

He shrugged unapologetically. 'I suspected.'

'Damn it.' Thanos shook his head. 'Why didn't you say something?'

'Because I couldn't be sure.' He leaned forward. 'You're the best person to run P & A, just like you've said time and again. I bought the company to keep it safe; I've never really considered Petó mine. As for P & A, there's no one else I'd rather pass it to.'

Thanos's breath hissed out of him with impatient frustration. 'All of this could have been avoided…'

'And you would have missed out on learning a very valuable lesson.'

'Oh, yeah? What's that? How to hurt innocent, beautiful, generous women?'

'On love,' Kosta corrected gently.

Thanos stood up with disbelief. 'You were, what? Trying to play matchmaker?'

Kosta's laugh was in complete contrast to the

darkness swirling through Thanos. 'I expected you would marry one of the party girls you're usually seen with,' Kosta corrected. 'I thought it would at least slow you down, that it might give you a wake-up call to stop partying, if not to show you how meaningful it can be to share your life with someone.'

'You were wrong on all counts!'

'Yes, because you chose Alice, and she loves you, and I do not think for one moment her feelings aren't mutual.'

'How do you know she loves me?' he muttered, wondering if they'd had some communication beyond what they'd shared on the island.

'Only a fool wouldn't have seen that,' Kosta said softly.

Thanos's heart was churning inside him, because the older man had a fair point. Only a fool wouldn't have seen… Had he realised and just refused to do anything about it?

'I came here to sign those contracts,' Thanos ground out, his heart banging so hard he thought it might burst right out of his chest.

'And we will,' Kosta promised. 'But let me say this, first.'

'I'm sick of talking about Alice,' Thanos groaned.

'Fine. This will be the end of it. Only, indulge an old man who liked and respected your grandfather; indulge an old man who likes you, Thanos, and doesn't want you to throw your life away because of stupid, stubborn fear.'

'Fear?' Thanos shook his head in silent dispute of that.

Kosta's voice came out gently. 'I know what it's like to live without the person you love. I lost my son.' His voice was just a hoarse whisper now, almost indiscernible above the distant rumbling of thunder and the crashing of the waves. 'I lost my wife. Neither of these things I had a choice in, but *you* do. Alice is out there, and she loves you, and you love her. All you have to do is reach out and grab her with both hands, and you're too damned afraid.'

Thanos stopped fighting the truth. He stopped fighting. He turned to face Kosta, his skin pale beneath his caramel tan. 'And what happens when she decides she doesn't love me after all?'

'And what happens if she doesn't?' Kosta threw back. 'What happens if you are a man like me in fifty years' time, staring out at the ocean and looking back on a lifetime of happiness and memories that you wouldn't trade an entire fortune for?'

Thanos listened to these words, his heart in his throat, Alice in his mind, and suddenly he felt it imperative to sign the papers and leave Kalatheros that had nothing to do with P & A and everything to do with somewhere else he desperately needed to be.

Running helped.

Alice had never been much of an athlete.

But after the grief and the depression and the desire to wallow had come a strange restlessness she hadn't been able to burn off. It made her legs twitch at night, while lying in bed, and her brain run like a freight train at all hours, so she would wake up in the middle of the night and be wide awake with no hope of sleep or rest.

She had a restlessness with nowhere to put her energy and so she'd taken up running. And not just running a little bit, either. She tried to do five miles morning and night.

It helped.

She didn't sleep better but her body was weary, so that she could lie on the sofa with mind-numbing television on in the background and try not to think about what her life would be like if she hadn't told Thanos how she felt.

Would they still be married? Sleeping together every night, her body wrapped around his, the sound of the waves that surrounded StathErá Prásino whispering in her ear, filling her soul with the beats of happiness?

Maybe.

Maybe not.

Maybe he would have sealed the deal with Kosta and put an end to things, finishing it because their marriage served no practical purpose.

Her chest felt heavy and strange at the very idea of that, and she knew she'd done the right thing. It was so much better to have left rather than to have been asked to leave.

She ran, one foot in front of the other, through Central Park then onto the busy streets surrounding it, weaving through people and bikes and cars and horse-drawn carriages stuffed with loud tourists; she ran with her head bent and her hair pulled into a plait, her earphones blocking out all the noise of the city she didn't care to hear.

And when she reached the foyer to the apartment he'd bought for her, which she'd eventually stopped fighting and accepted as a part of her life, she stopped running and pressed her hands to her knees, letting herself catch her breath for a few moments before she had to dredge up a smile and offer it to the doorman.

After just a moment she straightened and nodded in his direction as he held the glass doors open for her. The foyer was a testament to white marble and glass. Even in her rubber-soled sport shoes, she couldn't cross the space silently.

She pulled her earphones out as she approached the lift, jabbing the button with more anger than it deserved. Her breathing was still rushed. The doors opened and she stepped inside. The doors slid shut, except right as they were almost closed, just an inch or so from meeting in the middle, a hand slid between them, to hold them open. Alice fumbled, reaching behind her for the panel, looking for the 'door open' button.

It wasn't necessary. The hand succeeded. The doors opened and seconds later, as if her dreams and mind and hopes and heart had conjured him, Thanos swept into the lift.

CHAPTER FOURTEEN

SHE COULDN'T SPEAK.

There were a thousand words rushing through her, begging to be spoken, but she couldn't fumble her brain towards a single one of them in that second. She stared at him hungrily, her eyes refusing to obey and look away, her brain forgetting that he'd broken her heart and ceased to exist in her life, her heart chugging like a bouncing ball in her torso.

And he stared right back, his expression, his beautiful eyes moving with urgency over her face, as though he could somehow catalogue everything she'd done and said and felt in the three and a half months since she'd left the island.

She was in a state of shock, which was the only explanation for why it occurred to her to mind that she was wearing running gear, no make-up, and was covered in a sheen of perspiration from her exercise.

The lift began to cruise upwards and it was just the jolt Alice needed.

'Why are you here?'

His eyes glittered with determination. 'Isn't it obvious?'

Alice shook her head. 'Not to me.'

'I came to see you.'

Her heart lurched. 'Why?'

There was a brief hesitation. 'I have a favour to ask you.'

Alice groaned. 'A favour? Seriously?'

He nodded. The lift doors opened and Alice glared at him, contemplating telling him to get lost. But she didn't. She'd spent three and a half months wishing she could go back in time and eat her confession, wishing she could have just a bit more time with him.

She was furious with him. Furious with him for turning up in her apartment three and a half months after they'd last seen one another, blithely asking her for a favour.

But she was also human, and completely in love with Thanos, and desperate for whatever crumb of time she could steal. Even knowing it was just a temporary reprieve, that her grief would be waiting for her, that her reality wasn't any different.

He cast an eye about the apartment as he entered. She didn't offer him any refreshments. 'What do you want?'

Her tone was far from friendly.

He didn't react. 'Kosta and I have signed the

papers. He's in New York and asked if you were free to meet for a drink tonight, to celebrate. Champagne at the Stathakis hotel.'

Alice's heart dropped into her toes. 'Thanos,' she whispered, shaking her head as tears filled her eyes. 'You can't be serious?'

His expression was the most determined she'd ever seen it. 'I don't think I've ever been more serious about anything in my entire life.'

She spun away from him, swallowed desperately. 'Why?'

'Because you agreed to this, and it's not quite finished yet.'

Alice groaned, shaking her head. 'You said it was done.'

'I was wrong.'

Pain slashed through her.

'It's one hour,' he promised softly.

'One hour,' she said with disbelief. He couldn't understand her heartache, nor what he was asking of her. And yet…she thought of her mother and how well she was looking, of how her own life had changed since meeting Thanos, and she thought of the most important thing: none of this was his fault.

He'd been honest with her, even when she'd fallen in love with him, he'd tried to establish boundaries to make that impossible.

He hadn't set out to hurt her.

And she didn't want to hurt him. He needed one last favour.

With a sinking heart, and knowing how much this one hour would cost her, she found herself nodding. 'Fine.' Her voice was tremulous. 'But then, that's it. You go away again and forget I exist.'

His eyes glittered. 'Come to the hotel at six.' He reached into the breast pocket of his suit, pulling out a plastic key card. 'You remember the penthouse?'

Reluctance was awash through her central nervous system. 'Can't we meet in the bar?'

'No.' His eyes flared. 'You don't think that might tip Kosta off? Besides, I have your ring and necklace. You should wear them.'

This was a mistake.

Alice stared at her reflection in the mirrors outside the door to his penthouse, her body flashing with adrenaline as she studied her reflection.

She'd chosen a simple black dress, knee-length, figure-hugging, modest yet flattering, and teamed it with shiny black stilettos, the red sole a perfect match for the lipstick she'd chosen. Her dark hair had been brushed until it shone and left loose, if only because she knew he loved it that way.

Her fingers shook as she pulled the key card

from her handbag. But before she could insert it into the door, she knocked, preferring not to just let herself in.

When no one answered, she pressed the buzzer for the apartment and continued to wait.

Still no answer.

With a frown, she used the key card, and her frown didn't lessen when she stepped into the suite to find it in complete darkness.

'Thanos?' she called out, reaching around for a light switch. When she flicked it on, she made an audible sound of surprise that ricocheted off the walls.

'What the heck?'

The entire apartment was blanketed in red rose petals.

The *entire* apartment. It was like a red carpet, thick and luscious. She shook her head as she waded through them, her heart beating harder and faster, her mind unable to make any sense of it.

'Thanos?' Her voice was curt.

And she understood why she felt annoyed.

Because this didn't make sense.

And he shouldn't be here.

And this was too much.

And, and, and... Her body's defence mechanisms were firing to life, boarding up her too-soft heart, protecting her from the kinds of vulnerability that had led to her being hurt so badly.

A noise sounded and she shifted her focus, gasping once more when she saw what was beyond the balcony doors.

Candles.

Hundreds of candles.

Her heart slammed against her chest. She moved that way, closing her eyes as she stepped outside. Because there were roses there too, but long-stemmed red roses, so beautiful, so fragrant. She moved to one, feeling the petals, swallowing hard to clear the lump in her throat.

She spun around, her eyes searching for Thanos, and finally she found him. Standing on the deck, wearing a dark suit with no tie and a button undone at his neck, his eyes on her with such an intensity that a trail of heat pooled in her abdomen and ran all the way through her.

'I told Kosta the truth.'

The words didn't make sense. 'What?'

'I told him about us.'

'Why?' She shook her head. 'I thought you wanted P & A?'

'He's selling it to me anyway.'

'Oh.' She exhaled. 'Then why does he want to see me?'

Thanos's smile was just a twist of his lips. 'He doesn't.'

'What?' Nothing made sense and her blood

was pounding so hard in her ears she could barely hear anything above it.

'He's not in New York. I made it up.'

'Why?'

'I wanted to see you.'

She shook her head. 'You saw me earlier.'

'I wanted to see you properly. And for you to see me. Here. Like this.' He waved a hand around, gesturing to the roses and candles.

'What?'

She grimaced, knowing she sounded as if she had about two active brain cells and barely able to care. 'I don't get it.'

'I made a mistake.'

'When?'

He strode towards her and she clamped her mouth together, crossing her arms over her chest.

'I made a mistake when I let you go. I made a mistake every day I didn't look deep inside myself and see what was holding me back from you. I should never have let you leave.'

Alice was completely shocked. 'What?'

'I made a—'

'No.' She lifted a finger to his lips, silencing him, her eyes huge and beseeching. 'Don't you dare.'

Now it was Thanos's turn to look confused.

'Don't you dare think you can turn up after all this time—over three months—and say anything that's going to make this okay.' She glared at him, anger—the sweet relief of anger—everything she needed. 'Don't you dare think you can ever say or do anything that will make this all right.'

He lifted his hands and cupped her face, holding her still, holding her gently. 'I'm so sorry I hurt you.'

Except that.

His words were like treacle on her spine. 'Damn it.' She bit down on her lip, closing her eyes, but it did nothing to stop the tears from squeezing out of the corners.

'I'm sorry I didn't understand what we were. I'm sorry that you left and I felt like I'd been ripped into a thousand pieces and I *still* didn't see why. I'm sorry that I have been missing you and pining for you and thinking of you every day and it still didn't occur to me to realise that you have taken over my mind and soul in a way that is rare and beautiful and special.'

She sobbed, shaking her head and not really even knowing why.

'I'm sorry that I got so fixated on needing to control every single thing about us that I ruined it. I'm sorry that I hurt you, not once, but every single day that I stayed away. I'm sorry that I left you here thinking I don't love you when the truth is you are every breath in my body.'

She could barely breathe now, and her small sobs were little explosions firing from her.

'I'm sorry,' he continued, his own voice heavy with emotion, 'that I didn't understand what love was, what true love is, because I have never felt it before. But I get it now. I see how it is the way we fit together, the way we are together, the way I feel because of you—the fact you make me want to be a better man, a better person, you make me want to deserve you. You make me happier than I've ever known possible. I am so head over heels in love with you, *Kyria* Stathakis, and all I want is to tell you this.'

She blinked, her stomach rolling.

'That's not true,' he amended quickly. 'What I want is to make you my wife again, properly and for real. Not for show but because I do not want to go another day without you. What I want is to bring you back to the island, to have you at my side, not because we had a deal to fool a kind old man, or because I'm paying you, not because you are desperate for financial help and I offered that, but because you love me and I love you, and there is no way we should be anything other than together.'

Alice sobbed, her shaking head turning into a nod and then nothing as she tried to compute what was happening.

'I love you,' he said simply, his hands framing

her cheeks. 'And if you tell me I have ruined this beyond repair, I will try to prove you wrong. I will do whatever I can to fix this, for as long as it takes. I will be here, waiting, hoping, needing you but knowing I lost any right to expect you could possibly love me the day I let you walk out of my life.'

'Please don't,' she groaned, finally, tears in her voice. 'Please, just…'

'What?' His voice was gravelled. 'Tell me what I can do.'

She lifted her hands to his chest, staring at her splayed fingers, her eyes wide. 'I don't understand.' And she didn't, but it didn't stop her from believing and knowing. It didn't stop her from trusting.

'What do you not understand, *agape*?'

'What happened? Why are you here?' And then, softly, with a hint of accusation, 'It's been so long.'

'I know.' He pressed his forehead to hers. 'Too long. I was a fool, Alice Stathakis. Determined not to love you.' His eyes held hers, the truth in every fleck of them. 'I learned the flip side of loving someone at a young age, and I never forgot that pain.'

Alice's heart broke for the little boy he'd been, abandoned by his mother, made to feel unlovable, made to feel disposable.

'She was wrong to leave you,' Alice murmured. 'Wrong to let her little boy think he wasn't worthy of love; wrong to let you become a grown man who still believes that.'

And then his smile was blinding. 'But I don't believe it any more, Alice. Look what you did for me—look how you've loved me. Even tonight, after I broke your heart, you cared enough for me to come to my aid, to put your own pain aside because I asked it of you. There is no doubt in my heart that you love me, and that you will always love me.'

Alice blinked up at him, his words so beautiful, so perfect and all she wanted to do was reinforce that, to agree with him.

'And there is no doubt in my heart that I love you, and will always love you.' He brushed his lips over hers, just as he had the first time they'd kissed, and it sealed something inside her, filling her heart with all the joy she could possibly feel—and more, because she knew it was just the beginning.

'It was Kosta, you know,' Thanos murmured, stroking Alice's naked back, his fingertips revelling in the ability to touch her again so easily, his heart at peace for the first time in three and a half months.

Alice shifted a little in bed, the smile on her

lips that he would work the rest of his life to pre-serve, to earn. 'What was?'

'Who helped me see what an imbecile I was being.' He grimaced, but it was a grimace that was full of the fears that had gripped him—and the realisation of how close he'd come to ruining this for good.

'Did he, now?'

'Mmm…' It was a throaty noise of acknowl-edgement. 'He reminded me how lucky I am to have a chance to be with the person I love. Los-ing his wife hit him hard, and I think he looked at me, a man who was grieving the loss of someone I didn't have to lose, and he wanted to shake me.'

His smile was rueful.

'I'm glad.'

'Me too. Though I have to believe I would have woken up eventually. But who knows if you would have still been here by the time I saw things clearly?'

'I would have been,' she promised, entirely serious, no smile on her lips now. 'Thanos, I'm not going anywhere. Love isn't like that. When I told you I loved you, I meant it in a for-ever kind of way.' Heat flushed her cheeks. 'I gave you my heart with no expectation of ever getting it back.'

His eyes flared at her sweetness and he kissed her, slowly, hungrily, his whole body rejoicing in their closeness.

Later, over a pancake breakfast, he reached for Alice's hand, not liking how strange it was to see her finger without the engagement ring.

'I've been thinking,' he said quietly, 'about your mother.'

Alice's eyebrows shot up.

'Wherever we live, it should be near enough for us to see her often. I've made enquiries about having a space built on the island—fully staffed with nurses, of course—but I wanted to be sure you were happy with that. If you want to stay in New York, we can.'

Alice felt more love than she'd known possible burst through her. 'I think she—and I—would like nothing more than to live on your beautiful, sun-filled island, Thanos.'

He beamed. 'And so we shall.'

It took six months for construction to be completed, six months for world-class hospital staff to be recruited, and then they were back amongst the rolling green hills of Statherrá Prásino.

'The builders did a great job,' Alice said quietly, as they regarded the structure from a distance.

'Yes,' he agreed. 'It's close enough to the house, yet each building feels isolated and private.'

Alice tilted her head to the side, her pulse racing at the secret she'd been holding for just over a week. 'Do they do renovations as well? Or only new builds?'

'Why?' Thanos teased, wrapping his arms around his wife's waist. 'Do you fancy a remodelling project?'

'Only one room,' she said with a small smile.

'Yes?'

'I mean, it's not one hundred per cent necessary, but I thought a nursery would make it easier. You know, when the baby comes.'

'Whose baby?'

She burst out laughing. 'Ours, Thanos.'

'Our baby?'

She nodded, her eyes locked to his, her smile radiant on her face.

'Alice, do you mean…?'

She nodded, joy like a beacon glowing across the island. 'I'm pregnant!'

Thanos lifted her off the ground, spinning her around, momentarily lost for words. But when he put Alice's feet back on the sand, he knew just what he wanted to say. 'Thank you.'

She wrinkled her nose. 'What for?'

'For making me happier than I ever knew possible. Thank you for everything.'

The sun slipped into the ocean, the day drew to a close, but their lives lay before them: full of love, happiness, family and hope.

* * * * *